Break-ins and Bouquets
A Lexie Sarconi novel

G.K. Parks

and Elisa Archer

Copyright © 2015 Elisa Archer

© 2024 G.K. Parks

A Modus Operandi imprint

ISBN:
ISBN-13: 978-1-942710-42-4

For my muse

ONE

The flashing red and blue lights only made it worse. "Police," I announced, straining to hear over the sound of crunching glass beneath my boots.

"It looks like a smash and grab," Officer Kemper said. My partner for tonight's tour stopped to examine one of the destroyed display cases inside the jewelry store. "Whoever did this was in a rush."

"I don't think so." I pointed the beam of my flashlight at the large symbol spray-painted on the wall. "Most thieves don't stop mid-job to tag a place."

"It takes all kinds." Kemper moved away from the display case. "Didn't the security company say it was going to kill that alarm?" He peered skyward, squinting as the high-pitched squeal and flashing white lights continued going off.

"Get on the phone and get them to do it."

"C'mon, Lexie. You know I hate that part. Can't you see what's taking them so long?" Kemper stuck out his bottom lip.

Some days, I wondered why I wanted to be a cop.

"As soon as we finish clearing the place." Moving methodically through the store, I made a mental note of the number of smashed cases and the ones that remained intact as I searched the main area, behind the counters, and headed for the back.

Kemper followed behind. The narrow hallway led to several locked doors and offices. We checked each one. But the lack of broken glass and spray paint suggested the thieves hadn't been interested in whatever was kept back here. They were only interested in the shiny baubles and leaving a calling card. Why would they be so stupid?

"Keep an eye on the hallway," I said. "Just because we couldn't get into any of the rooms doesn't mean the thieves didn't."

"The locks would be broken, or the doors would be busted down. We would have noticed."

"Really?" I paused in the entryway, my hand on my radio. "Did you notice anything strange about the crime scene?"

"Besides the ugly mural?" Kemper pressed a finger to the paint. "It's still wet."

"Not that." Though the announcement sent chills through me. Whoever did this couldn't have gotten far. For all I knew, they could be right outside the door or locked inside one of the back offices. "They didn't break anything to get inside. Everything is intact. The door, the lock, all of it."

While I updated dispatch on the situation and made another request to the security company to turn off the alarm, I examined the locking mechanism more closely. No tool marks. Could the thieves have had a key?

Seconds before the blaring alarm turned off, a man in a blue hybrid pulled up to the building. He parked behind the police cruiser and hurried toward me. He had on a hoodie and pajama pants. He wore one slipper and one sneaker.

"What happened?" he shrieked over the alarm. "I received notification of a breach."

I held up my hand. "Sir, take a step back." I moved forward, hoping to prevent him from contaminating the scene.

"This is my shop."

"Can you show me some ID?"

He patted his pockets before tucking his hands into the front pouch of his hoodie. I tensed, more from training than because the man posed a threat. His sweatshirt didn't show the outline of a weapon, but it wasn't always possible to tell. "It's in the car." He tried to peer around me. "Can't I just go inside and see what happened?"

"Sir, your car's right there. And you left your door open and lights on."

He turned back to the vehicle. "Right. You're right." He rubbed his eyes and dashed back to his car. I kept an eye on him while he grabbed something off the passenger's seat, but it wasn't a weapon. It was his wallet. He had just turned off the lights and shut his door when an unmarked cruiser pulled up, followed by two more patrol cars.

The blaring alarm stopped, and Kemper let out a sigh of relief. "Finally."

I glanced at him. "Check the back doors again."

"We already did that," he griped. "Who put you in charge, anyway? We're both lowly patrol officers. You don't outrank me yet."

Before I could provide a snarky retort, Detective Lightman got out of the unmarked and approached me. "Officer Sarconi, I see you can't stay away from my crime scenes. Trying to butter me up in the hopes of claiming that slot in gangs?"

"Sir?"

"Where is it?"

"Where's what?"

Lightman stared at me like I was joking. But he knew we didn't have that kind of relationship. In fact, the last time I'd been tasked with helping his team, he'd made my life miserable to the point I almost wondered if he wanted me dead. Then he called a truce and offered me a permanent position with his team, once I made detective, if I made detective. "The graffiti."

I turned to see Detective Frank Devereaux had intercepted the shop owner, checked his ID, and was questioning him. Since I didn't have to work crowd control or maintain the crime scene now that a supervisor was here, I stepped back into the shop. "It's right there." I pointed the beam of my flashlight at the wall. "Kemper said it's still wet."

Lightman approached, appearing oblivious to everything else around him. His sole focus was on that hideous piece of street art. He stopped in front of it. "That's what I thought."

"What?"

The detective didn't turn to look at me. "You were first on scene."

"Yes, sir." I felt the need to answer, even though it hadn't been a question. "Officer Kemper and I responded to a call that the alarm was going off at this jewelry store. When we arrived, we found the front door open, those display cases smashed, and that on the wall. The back offices appear to be locked. No signs of tampering."

"They are locked," Kemper said. "We checked. Then I double and triple checked."

Lightman glanced at Kemper. "Was anyone here when you arrived?"

"No, sir. The place was empty. If someone had been here, I would have arrested his ass."

"Since you didn't get here soon enough to stop these guys, canvass the neighborhood. With the way the alarm was blaring, someone had to see something. Find out and make sure you let me know. I don't want either of you leaving this neighborhood until you locate at least one eyewitness. But I'd prefer three or four." Lightman spun away from the wall. "Get going."

Kemper moved toward the door, grumbling to himself. He must have forgotten what a pain in the ass Detective Lightman was. But I hadn't.

"Sir," I said, "there's one other thing. The front door doesn't show signs of a break-in."

"Did you check the back?"

"Interior only."

"You should check the back." He turned to face me. "Do that before you conduct the canvass. If you have something to report, use the radio. And keep an eye out. These guys may not have gotten far."

"Do you know who they are?"

Lightman expected to see the graffiti. For a gangs detective to respond to a break-in, this wasn't a run-of-the-mill smash and grab. Something else was going on here. But no one had briefed patrol. Perhaps the threat was new, it connected to an old case, or whatever this was was being kept under wraps for a reason.

"You don't want to know. Now get to work, Sarconi."

TWO

The back door to the jewelry store remained locked. No tool marks. No signs anyone had tried to gain entry.

"What do you think the graffiti was about?" I asked. "Have you seen that tag before?"

Kemper shook his head, miffed about our assignment. "Nope, but it sure was ugly."

"A skull with a crown," I said. "It must be a gang symbol. Lightman and Devereaux wouldn't be here otherwise."

"Maybe it was a slow night for gangs. Grand larceny could be busy or they just didn't want to be bothered. Since there's no body, RHD couldn't care less. Maybe Lightman drew the short straw, just like we did."

"Maybe." But I didn't think we drew the short straw. We were lucky. Patrol meant anything could happen. Compared to some of the things I'd seen, this was tame. I liked tame, especially at night when anything could happen.

Kemper led the way around the corner. We headed west, away from the store. But since this area was mostly offices and shops, no one was around this late at night. I made note of several security cameras, along with the business names and addresses.

Lightman would need that to collect the footage.

"I don't think we're going to find anything over here." I indicated the bright streetlights. "There's no cover. Guys running around in masks and carrying pillowcases with dollar signs drawn on them would be seen in a second. If the crooks came this way, they must have had a car waiting. They'd be long gone by now."

"Pillowcases with dollar signs." Kemper laughed. "This is why I like riding with you."

"I thought it was because you enjoy using me as your personal secretary." I gave him a scathing look. "You're an adult, Bobby. You can make your own phone calls."

Kemper quirked an eyebrow. "Damn, Lex, that's the first time you've called me by something other than my last name. You're making me tingle. Say my name again."

I gave him a playful shove. "Stop it."

"Say my name."

"Kemper."

"You're no fun."

"Haven't you realized that by now?"

"I was hoping something changed. You called me Bobby. That's gotta mean something. Are you reconsidering that standing invitation to grab a drink? If you play your cards right, I'll even throw in breakfast."

"Pass." I gave the cross street a careful look, but it was just as bright. I drew a tiny map in my notepad, complete with the streetlights and camera locations, making sure to indicate the cross streets and addresses before tucking it away and reversing course.

"I seem to recall you referring to Detective Riley by his first name on several occasions. What makes him so special?"

Not dignifying that with a response, I crossed at the intersection, even though traffic was non-existent, and headed back the way we came so I could repeat the checks on this side of the street. "Do you think we'll find an eyewitness?"

"It depends. Normally, a few unhoused hang around. With the right incentive, we may be able to get them to offer up an account."

"Are you sure? There are no encampments around here."

"I'm counting on a few loners or stragglers. If not, we'll be walking these streets for the rest of our lives. Lightman's never gonna let us off this call until we bring him what he wants."

"He knew the graffiti would be there." I considered the possibilities. "Someone's done this before." I'd have to check gang symbols. "The skull and crown could be their calling card, the way they mark their territories. And it's still wet."

"I told you that," Kemper said.

"How long does spray paint take to dry?"

"About ten minutes."

"Whoever did this must be close. We barely missed him." I picked up the pace, checking each alleyway we passed. "Given the colors used, he had at least six cans with him. Those would fit in a backpack or bag."

"Don't forget his loot."

Jewelry didn't take up a lot of space, and it wasn't fragile. The thief or thieves could have tossed it into the same bag as the cans of spray paint. If they were smart, professional street artists, or had done it before, they would have known to wear masks to avoid inhaling the paint mist and fumes. Someone must have seen them escaping.

We made it back to the jewelry store. By now, Sunshine Security had arrived. Detective Frank

Devereaux gestured to the door and the posted cameras while he spoke to the tech. Lightman was questioning the store owner near the back corner. Patrol officers had roped off the interior while they waited for the crime lab to arrive.

Officers Hawking and Sanchez were checking nearby dumpsters. From the looks of it, they weren't having any luck either.

"Did Lightman assign you to dumpster dive?" Kemper asked.

Hawking glanced up. "We're looking for the paint cans. Did you find anything?"

"Not yet. We're supposed to be searching for witnesses," I said.

"Ten says you have better luck than we do," Kemper said.

"I wouldn't count on it." Hawking hoisted himself into the dumpster, cringing when his boots made a squishing sound.

"Why do you think I only wanted to put ten on it?" Kemper asked.

"Good luck," I said to Hawking. "If you happen to see or hear anything, let us know. The suspects may still be in the area. Keep an eye out."

"Will do, Sarconi."

We moved away from the store, continuing our canvass eastward. "Looks like the band's getting back together." Kemper shone his flashlight into an alcove, causing a rat to make a chittering sound and scurry away. I jumped at the sound and movement. "Maybe Lightman will ask us to assist his team again."

"Is that something you really want to do?" I asked.

"I don't know. Detective Preston wasn't too bad. I liked working with her. Nice legs. Nice ass."

"She won't sleep with you," I said.

"Why not? Her reputation suggests otherwise."

"You're a puppy, Kemper. She's only interested in the big dogs."

"Game recognizes game?"

"You're the one who said she wants to sleep her way to the top."

I slowed as we approached the next intersection. Traffic cams covered every direction in the four-way. If the thief came this way, he had to be on the footage. I reached for my radio, letting Lightman know this would be a good place to start. Then I chose a direction and turned left.

Going left gave me the creeps with all the dark shadows and fewer storefronts. This way led to overpasses, empty lots, and parking structures. If anyone was out, unhoused or otherwise, this is where they'd be if they didn't want to be seen or bothered.

"It'd serve you better to learn from her than to try to seduce her. Preston's a badass and a brilliant cop. She'll make you a better cop."

Kemper snorted. "Is that what you tell yourself about Riley?"

I didn't answer.

"C'mon, Lex. It's just us out here. Be honest. Something's going on with the two of you. I see the way he looks at you, and the way you look at him. He's why you turned me down."

"Nothing's going on between me and Riley."

"I don't believe you."

"I don't care what you believe." I froze in front of an alleyway. The hairs at the back of my neck prickled.

"Now wh—"

I held up my hand, warning Kemper to be quiet. Someone or something was down there. After signaling to him again, I placed my flashlight beneath my weapon and kept it aimed at the ground as I stepped into the alleyway.

Splotches of orange paint made a path. There hadn't been any paint on the sidewalk. But there was paint here. I pointed to it, scanning the walls surrounding us for more tagging and graffiti, but I didn't see anything fresh. Kemper pushed ahead of me, his gun out and aimed in front of him.

The paint trail led to a dumpster. Reaching out with his non-dominant hand, Kemper flipped the lid open. It banged against the brick wall, making the metal rattle.

A high-pitched wail sounded from the other end. A garbage can crashed to the ground. The metal clang echoed against the walls. Movement caught my eye. A flash of white, then nothing more than a shadow.

I aimed.

"Relax. It's a cat." Kemper gave the area in front of us one more look before peering into the dumpster. "What happens if we find the spray paint? Does that mean Hawking and Sanchez have to find eyewitnesses?" Kemper holstered his weapon and leaned over the dumpster. "I can almost reach it."

But something else had moved. What I saw wasn't a cat. I took a few more steps forward, my gun and flashlight aimed low. The paint trail didn't stop at the dumpster. It continued.

This didn't feel right. If the cans were leaking, we would have seen paint on the sidewalk. Kneeling down, I pressed my gloved fingers to the paint. It was fresh.

This was a trap. But we'd already walked into it. Pressing my shoulder to the wall, I kept my eyes focused in front of me, my head on a swivel. A tarp was draped over the dumpster near the other end of the alley. It stretched across to some old buckets, almost like a makeshift tent.

"Police," I identified myself. "Show yourself. Hands

up."

"What are you doing?" Kemper dropped the dumpster lid, making me jump. "It was a fucking cat."

"Show yourself," I repeated, moving closer to the tarp.

The orange paint drops stopped in front of the next dumpster. I didn't look inside. Instead, I continued past it, hoping Kemper would provide backup. Keeping one eye on the dumpster, I barely noticed the tarp swaying.

"Lexie, check this out," Kemper said, opening the second dumpster and leaning in. "I found more spray paint." He stood on his tiptoes, folding over the side and straining to reach the discarded can.

"No. Don't." But I was too late.

Whoever had been hiding behind the dumpster shoved it forward, rolling the heavy metal into my partner and knocking him inside. The lid slammed down, trapping Kemper.

Before I could react, someone rushed at me. The tarp prevented me from seeing the suspect. I raised my flashlight and gun, but he was on top of me before I could think to do anything. All I could see was the gritty, blue tarp. It clung to me. Whoever had been hiding behind it tangled me inside of it.

A loud bang sounded, followed by metallic echoing. Something had hit the dumpster hard. Maybe Kemper had gotten out. I clawed and fought until I was free of the tarp. I caught a glimpse of a man's back disappearing onto the street.

Stumbling, I unlocked the lid on the dumpster. "Are you okay?"

Kemper looked rattled, but he nodded.

"Radio he's headed west on Seventeenth." Then I raced after the suspect. I was fast. But he had too much of a head start. Pumping my arms as fast as I could in the hopes my legs would move even faster, I watched as he turned down the next street.

I ran even faster, my eyes watering and my breath coming in heaving gasps. By the time I made that turn, a red car was driving away. From this distance, I couldn't make out the plates.

"Shit." I put my hands on my head and tried to slow my breathing. My heart pounded in my ears, my legs cramping from the sudden start and stop. I continued moving forward. No paint spatter. No dropped jewelry. Nothing indicated the man who set up that ambush in the alleyway was the same guy who escaped in the red car. But it had to be the same guy. There was nowhere else for him to go.

Diagonally across the street, past the next intersection, was a food truck. It was too late for him to be in service. Cautiously, I approached, my breathing barely under control. When I rapped on the window, the door at the back opened. Already edgy, I put my hand on my gun and gave the vehicle a wide berth.

"Officer," he exhaled, "is this about parking illegally or the guy who just outran you?"

"Why are you here?" I asked, already suspicious.

"Engine trouble. The damn thing broke down when I was on my way back to the lot. The tow guy said two hours. It's been four."

"I'll see if I can get that expedited for you, but first," I pointed, still struggling to catch my breath, "tell me what you saw."

THREE

Detective Lightman rubbed his hand over his face. "It's not much. Is that really all you found, Sarconi?"

"No one else was out. If they were, they took off before we got to them."

"A lot of that going around." Lightman watched the tow truck driver secure the wheels of the food truck with chains. "Your eyewitness didn't see the guy break into the jewelry store. He didn't see anything useful."

"He saw him flee the scene."

Lightman put his hands on his hips and sighed dramatically. "He saw him flee the alleyway where you and Kemper were playing in the trash."

"That bastard set a trap. He lured us there with the spray paint." I narrowed my eyes. "Why would a thief do that? He stole the jewelry, left his calling card, and got away without being seen. Why would he stop there?"

"Beats me." But I didn't believe a word Lightman said. "You and Kemper can return to the station, write your reports, make sure I get a copy, and call it a night. Your shift ended hours ago. I already cleared your OT with the watch commander and Lt. Peterson. You're welcome."

Without waiting for our inevitable protests, Lightman went to join Detective Devereaux at the food truck.

Kemper yawned. "You heard the man. Let's go, Lexie."

I gave the alleyway one last look. A forensics unit was checking for evidence inside the dumpsters and near the tarp. I wondered what they'd find. Once we were back inside our patrol car on the way back to the station, I asked, "Does any of this make sense to you?"

"Sure."

"Sure?"

"Yeah. We chased down the guy, who must have heard the sirens and feared he'd get caught, so he hid in the alley. He went to dump the evidence, but the orange paint can was leaking. That's how you found his hiding spot. Two of the other paint cans were in that first dumpster. I don't know why he wanted to spread them out, but he did. Maybe he tossed the others into another dumpster in another alley. People panic. They don't want to get caught."

"You only found three cans? Not six?"

"Like I said, he could have ditched them anywhere," Kemper repeated.

"Fine." But I didn't believe it. "How did he get inside the jewelry store?"

"Maybe the owner forgot to lock up. I mean, the guy did leave his car door wide open and his lights on when he arrived."

"He was half-asleep and freaked out. He wasn't thinking."

"He had on one shoe, Lex. And he's old. Maybe the elevator doesn't go all the way to the top anymore."

"He wasn't that old."

"Some people start losing it young."

"Like you?"

Kemper shook his head. "Sometimes, you're a real bitch."

I sucked in a breath. My gut instinct was to snap at him, but we were both tired and coming down from the adrenaline surge. Snapping wouldn't help matters. Maybe I was reading this situation wrong. "I don't like feeling trapped. That's how I felt in that alleyway."

"How do you think I felt when I got stuck in that nasty dumpster?" Kemper glanced at me from the corner of his eye. "Is that phobia a remnant from your days working vice?"

"It's not a phobia. I just don't like being stuck somewhere with no way out. But some asshole who's brazen enough to go after cops doesn't bode well. Can we at least agree on that?"

Kemper nodded. "I'm sorry I called you a bitch. I get it. It was a rough shift and a half. I'm glad it's over."

"Me too."

"So what do you say to that drink? We earned it."

I shook my head. "We both could use a shower and some sleep." I pointed at him. "Not together."

He chuckled. "So you are thinking about it."

After finishing the paperwork, we called it a night. After two weeks of this, I was sick of working nights, especially when we always ended up getting a call right at the end, which guaranteed we'd be stuck working hours longer than we planned. At least the OT was good, but I missed having a life. The detective's exam was fast approaching, and I could have used the extra time to study or sleep. Hopefully, tomorrow would be better.

The sky started to brighten as I parked in front of my apartment building, but it did nothing to improve my mood. Working nights sucked. What sucked even more was that my schedule was opposite Detective

Michael Riley's. At least we had a little bit of time before he had to go to work. I looked at the clock. Three hours. But he'd be asleep for most of it, and I didn't want to wake him just because I had a crappy day. We hadn't been dating long enough for that. That was acceptable at six months, but we'd only been together less than three.

Let it go, Lexie. I should consider myself lucky to not be working for vice. At least the police uniform was better than the outfits I'd worn as a decoy hooker. That felt like a lifetime ago. A lot had changed, and yet, nights like this made me realize things hadn't changed enough.

After unlocking my apartment door, I couldn't help but smile at the man asleep in my bed. Michael was right. Sleepovers were a must, or we'd never see one another. Quietly, I padded into the bathroom. The only thing I wanted to do was wash that nasty alleyway and those dumpsters off me.

I turned on the water and stripped down, placing my dirty uniform and the clothes I'd worn on the ride home in a trash bag. I'd have to do laundry before going to work if I didn't want my entire apartment to reek. More things to add to the to-do list. Hopefully, the laundry room would be quiet, so I could study while my clothes were getting cleaned.

Once I was freshly showered, having washed off the grime and annoyance of the night, I wrapped a towel around me and dried my hair. The bathroom door creaked open, and I froze, my nerves shot from my last tour.

"Lex, can I come in?"

Turning off the hair dryer, I secured the towel a little tighter and pushed open the bathroom door. "I didn't mean to wake you. Go back to sleep. You have to get up soon."

A smile tugged at Michael's lips. "I'm up now." He pulled me to him for a kiss.

"I see what you mean."

He lifted me onto the vanity and nuzzled against my neck. The stubble on his jaw tickled my bare skin. "I wish I'd woken up sooner. I could have surprised you in the shower." He stepped back. "Are you okay?"

"The last call was a weird one."

"Do you want to talk about it?"

"I just want to go to bed."

"Good answer." He threw me over his shoulder, making me squeal. When we reached the bed, he dropped me into the middle of the warm sheets. "I've been waiting all night for this." He pounced, making me giggle. "I wonder what's underneath the towel."

"Nothing."

He quirked an eyebrow. "I'm a detective. I'll have to investigate for myself."

"I bet you use that line on all the ladies."

"You're the only one, babe." He stole another kiss, his fingers on the tucked in top of the towel.

I stared up at him as he sat back, a satisfied grin on his face as he slowly undid my towel and separated the two ends. The anticipation sent shivers through me. He lowered his lips to my neck, kissing downward.

"Michael," I breathed.

"Shh. I'm just getting started."

I wrapped my arms around him, never wanting to let go. He stopped what he was doing and looked me in the eye.

"Hey," he brushed a strand of hair out of my face, "what's going on?"

I shook my head. "Don't worry about it. It's nothing important."

He gave me an uncertain look and reared back,

breaking free of the grip I had on him and pulling his t-shirt over his head. Then he wrapped me in his arms and rolled us over, so I was on top.

Pressing my cheek against Michael's toned chest, I let the sound of his heartbeat drone out the thoughts in my head, the million things I had to do before next shift, and the million questions I had concerning the jewelry store break-in. Michael Riley always knew exactly what I needed. He smelled like soap, my laundry detergent, and something all him.

I kissed a line across his chest and down his sternum. He ran his fingers through my hair, watching as I placed sloppy kisses against his washboard abs. Once he was sure my mind was focused on the task at hand, he flipped us back over and continued where he left off.

Unfortunately, that was short-lived when something buzzed across the nightstand. I let out an exhale, my mind back on work. "Yours or mine?"

"Mine." Michael checked the display, gave me one more kiss, and took his cell phone into the living room.

"Stupid job."

I grabbed his t-shirt from the bottom of the bed and pulled it on before snuggling under the covers. Calls like that meant one thing. He had to leave. We'd have to finish this another time. At this rate, maybe we could pencil in a few minutes sometime next year.

The pillow smelled just like him, and I buried my face in it and closed my eyes. A few minutes later, he grabbed his bag off the chair and went into the bathroom. When he emerged, he smelled like mouthwash and aftershave. He was dressed in jeans and a henley, not his usual dress shirt.

"Lexie," Michael whispered in my ear as he leaned over the bed and kissed my cheek, "I have to go. Jack called. He needs me to check something out."

"The jewelry store."

"How do you know that?"

"I was there."

Michael's expression changed. "You were there? What were you doing there? Are you okay?"

"I'm fine. Kemper and I responded to a call from the alarm company. I don't know how the hell the thief got inside. He must be a relative of Harry Houdini." I shook my head. "That bastard."

"But you're okay?"

"Yeah. Lightman made us canvass for eyewitnesses. We tracked down the suspect, or at least I think we did, but he got away."

Michael gave me another hug, burying his face in my hair before giving me a kiss. "Jack didn't mention you were there."

"Why would he?" A frightening thought came to mind. "He doesn't know about us, does he? We said we were waiting to make sure before we disclosed. You didn't file paperwork without me, did you?"

"God no. I wouldn't do that, especially with the detective's exam looming. I'd never do anything to jeopardize your chances at a promotion. You know I want you off the street more than anyone."

But there was something he wasn't saying. "Why would Lightman mention I was there?"

"I figured he might. We worked together. He invited you to join our team. I... I don't know what I was thinking." Michael ran a hand through his dark hair, making it do that sexy spiky thing I liked so much. "You have me twisted around. All the blood hasn't returned to my brain yet."

"If you stay a few more minutes, I bet we can fix that."

"That is so tempting," he gave me another kiss, "but

I have to go."

"Do you have time for coffee? I can make some."

"No, honey. Stay where you are. I want you to get some sleep. Since you're riding with Kemper, you need to be well-rested so you'll be awake and alert. I don't trust that guy not to do the stupidest shit."

"He's not that bad." Thoughts of the alleyway and Kemper getting trapped inside the dumpster came to mind, but sharing that with Michael would only make him worry more.

"No, he's worse." Michael moved away from the bed, stopping in front of my mirror to button the bottom buttons on the henley. His taut, sinewy muscles bunched as his hands moved effortlessly over the material. His blue eyes sparkled, and his gorgeous lips formed a playful grin. "Like what you see?"

"I'd like it better if it was under the covers. When are you getting a day off?"

"That depends on what turned up—" Michael shut his mouth. "We shouldn't be discussing this."

"The jewelry store break-in?" I pointed to the dresser. "Check my notepad before you go. I might have written down something useful. I mapped out the nearby cameras and marked where the suspect hunkered down."

"Hunkered down?"

"I thought he set a trap. Kemper thinks he was waiting for the heat to die down before escaping."

Michael picked up the notepad and flipped the pages, scanning as he went. "This is the only description of the suspect?"

"That's all I got."

"And this is the location where you found him?" He held up the next page of my notes.

"Yeah, but I didn't get a good look. By the time I was able to give chase, he was too far away. The only eyewitness we found provided a better description of the getaway vehicle, but not of the man."

Michael closed the notepad and put it back on my dresser. "That's not what I expected. I'll have to check it out. See what's what. If I don't see you before you start your shift, be careful."

"You too."

"I'm always careful." He clipped his handcuffs, shield, and gun to his belt and put on his jacket. "Get some sleep, Lexie. With any luck, I'll be back before you wake up." He palmed my spare key. "I'll lock your deadbolt on my way out."

"You don't have to. I am armed."

"I'll do it anyway. It'll make me feel better."

"Didn't we talk about that overprotective thing?"

"I'm not overprotective. I'm cautious."

"You're a hotshot detective. You throw caution to the wind."

"Not when it comes to you."

"See," I pointed at him, "overprotective."

FOUR

I stared at the neon glow from the digital clock. I'd slept through my alarm, so I didn't have time for laundry or studying. I hated working nights. After eating breakfast or maybe it was dinner since it was hard to keep up given my crazy sleep schedule, I filled my travel cup with coffee and headed for the station. I found Officer Kemper waiting for me.

"Hey, Lexie," he called, "did you finish your report from last night's break-in?"

"Yeah, why?" I glanced toward the lieutenant's office. "Did Peterson not get a copy of something?"

"I don't know, but the brass was bitching about the jewelry store heist. I don't know what's going on. I was afraid it was something we had done."

"We didn't do anything."

"You let the suspect get away."

"Me?"

Kemper sighed. "We, but it really wasn't our fault. He got the drop on us. What were we supposed to do?"

There were a lot of things we should have done, starting with better communication. If Kemper had believed me or if I'd said something more direct, maybe we would have been able to apprehend the suspect. That must have been why the brass was pissed. This wouldn't bode well for my evaluation.

I blinked a few times. "Did you say heist? It was a smash and grab."

"Heist is what Lt. Peterson called it."

"How can breaking inside and smashing the display cases be considered a heist?"

"Don't ask me," Kemper said. "I'm only repeating what I heard."

"Was something else taken? Did the thief empty a safe?"

Kemper shrugged.

"A heist implies planning, premeditation, careful prep." I thought about the lack of damage to the front door. "Do they think this was an inside job?"

"I don't know, Lex." Kemper's lips curled into a smile. "But Lightman may need some help with this. Maybe we can get out of patrolling and assist the investigation. You and me were at the scene. Gangs already knows we can get the job done after the last time we were temporarily reassigned to help out. Maybe you could ask Detective Riley to put in a good word for us."

"You really want to work with Riley again?"

"I'd prefer Preston, but Riley and I are cool now. It's all good."

I didn't want to burst Kemper's bubble, but Michael couldn't stand him. The reason being me. I'd never had men fight over me before. While in theory it seemed like something out of a fairytale, the reality was anything but. I didn't like being thought of as a prize, even though Michael insisted that hadn't been his motivation. I still wasn't sure that was true, but he knew better than to pull that macho shit again. I wouldn't tolerate it. He had to respect me as a cop first and foremost, which was why I wasn't sure we should work together on this case or any case.

"If you want to volunteer, you talk to Riley or Lightman. I'm keeping my head down and my nose clean. I don't want to make waves or ask for favors. Rocking the boat is not something we should be doing weeks before the exam. You know the brass is watching us. Any misstep could trip us up on getting promoted," I said.

"You've got that backwards, Lexie. Now's the time to show initiative. Demonstrate you aren't afraid of hard work or tough cases."

"We let a suspect escape."

"That's not how I see it," Kemper said. "Through sheer determination, we were able to track him down and identify his getaway vehicle."

"Because he got away."

"There's no talking to you." He leaned in. "It's all about spin."

"Whatever you say." I didn't care about spin. I cared about the case and making sure my partner and I followed protocol.

I looked around the roll call room, hoping to spot Michael. Since he hadn't returned to my apartment before I had to leave for work, he must have gotten bogged down. But he wasn't lingering near the podium, preparing to brief patrol on the case or ask for volunteers to assist gangs. I wasn't sure who was more disappointed by this, me or Kemper.

"Hey." Officer Hawking took a seat beside us. "Do you have any idea why the white shirts think the incident at the jewelry store is more than a run-of-the-mill break-in? No one was hurt. No one was even there."

"It's the graffiti on the wall," I said, "and the ease of entry."

"The lab didn't pull any prints off the spray paint

cans. I don't think they found any evidence at the crime scene either." Hawking looked around. "Sanchez heard gangs was investigating the alarm company."

"Inside job?" I asked.

"That's how it reads. The graffiti may be to throw us off the scent."

"What about the security footage?" Kemper asked. "The jewelry store had plenty of cameras inside."

"No one mentioned anything to me. But that's above my paygrade." Hawking was usually not one to gossip.

"Why bring it up?" I asked.

Hawking jerked his chin toward the windows where we could see Detective Lightman emphatically gesturing at something Lt. Peterson was holding in his hand. "On my way in, I heard your names, specifically Lightman sharing your escapades in the alley with the LT."

"Good or bad?" I asked.

Hawking tilted his head to the side. "I'm sure it's not that bad."

"What did you write in your report?" I asked Kemper.

"I said how it went down. I wouldn't jam you up, Lex. What did you write?"

I narrowed my eyes. Kemper had a reputation for running off half-cocked. He didn't think things through. Instead, he'd react. That's how he ended up stopping an armed robbery by himself while off duty his first week on the job. He never called for backup. He was a glory hog. Did he think of me as his competition for the detective's spot?

"I just wrote the facts," I said.

"Okay, Joe Friday."

I chuckled. Hawking had always been the Joe

Friday figure in our group. Before I could say anything else, Lightman appeared in the doorway, his arms crossed in front of his chest.

"Sarconi and Kemper, I need to see you." Lightman didn't wait for us to respond before turning and walking out of the room.

"Sir?" I asked, hurrying to catch up to Lightman who was on his way back to the gangs unit.

As soon as we entered through the double doors, Lightman stopped and turned. He glanced over my head, making sure we hadn't lost Kemper, before he said, "The two of you are going back to that neighborhood. I told you I expected you to find several eyewitnesses. You barely found one and what he has to say won't help me in any way, shape, or form."

"What about the make of the getaway vehicle or the description he provided?"

Lightman sucked in a breath and scratched his brow, fighting to keep his annoyance in check. "You mean the stolen car we found abandoned a mile away with no prints or trace we can use? Or the vague description of a figure in black running away from you, Officer Sarconi?"

"Sir—"

"Save it, Sarconi." Lightman turned his inscrutable stare on Kemper. "What did you bring me?"

"I...um..." Kemper swallowed. "We found the spray paint and where the thief was hiding."

"Thief?" Lightman shook his head, his eyes going skyward while he mumbled to himself. "You have no idea what is going on here."

"Why don't you tell us." I kept my tone low. Respect wasn't one of my strong suits until it was earned.

"You're patrolling tonight. Find me something

worthwhile, and I'll think about reading you in." Lightman jerked his chin toward the door. "Get going."

"Yes, sir." Kemper pushed open the door.

"Didn't you offer me a spot on your team?" I asked Lightman.

"You never accepted. If you want me to offer it again, you have to earn it."

Backing away, I spotted Michael in the conference room. Detective Frank Devereaux was beside him, but I couldn't see where Devereaux was pointing. At least that explained why Michael hadn't made it back to my apartment before I left for work and why I hadn't caught a glimpse of him near the roll call room. He was stuck working a double because of whatever went down in the jewelry store.

"Sarconi," Lightman called before the door closed, "be vigilant."

His words made the hairs on the back of my neck stand at attention. Lightman rarely provided warnings. Whatever this was had to be serious.

~*~

Kemper drove with one hand on the wheel, the other drumming a rhythm against the door. "It looks like we're pulling double duty, regular patrol while working for Detective Lightman. I don't see why he gets preferential treatment? He's a Detective III. So what if he runs his own unit? Who cares? That doesn't make him super cop or put him in charge of us. We aren't in his chain of command."

"Refresh my memory. Didn't you say something about wanting to assist gangs?"

"Only if we didn't have to work patrol too. I don't want to do both." Kemper shook his head. "This feels punitive."

"Isn't it?"

"We responded to a call. We secured the scene. No one was there when we arrived. We had no way of knowing where the thief had gone or how much of a head start he had on us. If we'd immediately started searching for him, we would have been reprimanded for that. We had to wait."

"It doesn't matter," I said. "Whatever this thief did has the attention of the gangs unit. That means we aren't looking at a thief or a break-in. We're looking at something else. I'm guessing it has to do with the graffiti on the wall. Any idea whose tag that is?"

"Nope."

"We should assume it's a gang tag, otherwise Lightman wouldn't be in charge of the investigation."

"Agreed." Kemper drove past the jewelry store. The lights were off, but from the outside, it didn't look like it had been the scene of a crime. No exterior damage. "I didn't notice any street art or tags on other buildings in this neighborhood. These are almost all businesses." He continued straight. "Not a lot of activity here at night."

"What about up there?" I pointed to a section of illuminated signs.

"Fast-food joints. A couple of diners. A twenty-four hour pharmacy. A convenience store." Kemper chuckled. "A sex shop."

I glanced down at the GPS. "Lucky for us, all of that is still in our patrol zone."

"So what?"

"We didn't check any of these places last night because we assumed the thief would flee from the crowd, not go toward them."

Kemper wasn't following. "It'd be stupid to go toward them with pockets full of stolen jewelry. Plus, we found him holed up in that alley. He wasn't anywhere near here."

"The paint had to come from somewhere. Maybe he stopped for a burger before pulling the job. Or maybe someone inside one of these places knows something about which gangs operate in the area."

"You want to investigate gang activity?"

"You said I needed to show initiative. What do you say?"

Kemper pulled into a parking space in between a fast-food restaurant and the pharmacy. "Fine, but if we don't find Lightman's eyewitnesses, you're taking the hit."

I got out of the car, checked to make sure the volume on my radio was turned up so I'd hear any incoming calls, and gave Kemper a look over the roof of the car. "Did you miss the lectures at the academy on teamwork?"

"We are a team, but this is your idea. If it doesn't pan, you should take the hit."

"What happens if we bust this thing open and find someone who can ID the thief and lead us right to him?"

"You get the credit. It was your idea."

"That's how you want to do this?"

"It's only fair." Kemper looked at his watch. "We pursue this until we take lunch, or until we get a call. Afterward, we do what I want."

"Which is?"

"I'll let you know."

FIVE

We spoke to plenty of people, but no one had anything to say about the jewelry store break-in or area gang activity. Detective Lightman had already secured the relevant surveillance footage. If there was anything to learn, he should have it at his disposal.

"Now what do you want to do?" Kemper asked, checking the time. "Your first idea was a bust."

"I know that," I hissed.

Kemper chuckled and bumped against my shoulder. "I'm just messing with you. Lightman gave us a shit assignment yesterday, and he's punishing us by making us repeat it today."

"In that case, let's go back to the scene of the crime."

"The jewelry store?" Kemper raised an eyebrow. "The place is locked up." He pointed to the seal on the front of the door. "It's still being evaluated for evidence."

"If that were true, an officer would be stuck babysitting it."

"I'm surprised Lightman didn't make us do that." Kemper exhaled.

"Either way, I don't want to go back inside the

jewelry store. I want to go back to the alleyway where the suspect got the jump on us. This time, don't tell me it's nothing more than a cat."

"I doubt anyone will be hiding in the shadows a second time." I gave Kemper a look, and he held up his palms. "Fine. I won't tell you it's a cat or rat. I'll follow your lead for the next twenty-eight minutes. Then we're taking lunch," he said.

"Agreed." I marched down the street, giving the buildings we passed a more thorough look. Last night, I'd been in a rush to see if we could track the suspect. Tonight, I wondered if we missed something.

Besides several scary shadows and the disgusting smell of trash and urine, there weren't any clues or evidence between the jewelry store and the alleyway. Not a single droplet of paint had fallen onto the sidewalk. No paint smudges from shoes or splashes of color. I pointed it out to Kemper.

"It doesn't mean it's a trap. Maybe he didn't take the orange can out until he got near those dumpsters. That's why the paint only spilled there," Kemper reasoned.

"I'm not so sure." I swept my flashlight from left to right as I entered the alleyway. This time, I didn't spot any stray cats. The tarp was gone, eliminating the few hiding places that had existed. "Did they get any prints off the tarp?"

"Hawking said no," Kemper reminded me.

"And nothing on the cans either."

"The suspect was obviously wearing gloves. He wouldn't want to leave prints in the store or get paint on his hands."

"I guess not." Crouching down, I pointed to the paint smears.

"That wasn't sprayed. It dripped." Kemper knelt beside me. "If the suspect had sprayed it to trick us or trap us, it'd be lighter around the edges and concentrated in the middle. This is more like a droplet."

"A big droplet."

"Maybe the can got pierced or the tip was leaking. Either would explain this." Kemper stood up, wiping his palms on his pants. "It looks accidental to me."

Slowly, I swept my flashlight around the alley again. The dumpsters had been dusted and anything that could have been considered evidence had been collected. But something caught my eye. Getting up, I approached the dumpster where Kemper had gotten trapped.

The previous night's events played through my mind, particularly the loud bang and metallic echoing. Opening the lid on the dumpster, I shone my light through the tiny hole. The beam entered the hole in the front of the dumpster, shone solid against the dark interior, and came out a slightly larger hole on the other side of the dumpster.

"Lex," my name caught in Kemper's throat, and he swallowed, "you don't think..."

"You tell me. You were inside that thing." I went around to the back of the dumpster and examined the exit hole. The metal had been pierced from the inside out, unlike the hole in the front, which had been pierced from the outside in.

"Everything got really loud. Lots of reverb, but I thought he had banged against the outside. I don't recall hearing a gunshot. Do you?"

"I heard a bang." I searched the brick wall behind the dumpster, finding a spot where the brick had been chipped away. Dust filled the space and had formed a tiny pile on the ground below. Forensics had found the bullet and dug it out of the wall. But I wasn't sure why no one had told us about it or asked about it. "It didn't sound like a gunshot. But it must have been."

"That could be old," Kemper said. "We know what gunfire sounds like. We would have recognized it."

I checked the holes in the dumpster again. "No rust. This is fresh."

"It doesn't mean it happened last night."

I wasn't sure if Kemper was in denial about the close call or he couldn't believe we wouldn't have been told or questioned about it.

He put his hands on his hips and gave the rest of the alleyway a careful perusal. "I'm starving. Can we go to lunch now?"

"You want to eat after this?" I pointed to my latest revelation.

"Yeah. What does this have to do with me? If the asshole last night had a gun, we would have heard the shot. It's that simple."

"What if he had a suppressor?"

"We still would have heard it. The acoustics here would have made it go boom."

"Something went boom. I didn't know what the sound was."

Kemper kicked the dumpster. "It was that."

"No, it wasn't." I reached for my radio, but Kemper grabbed my hand.

"Lexie, stop. If the suspect lured us here, like you think he did, and had a gun, he wouldn't have shoved me in a dumpster and shot the dumpster. He would have shot me and you. The fact that we're still breathing means he didn't have a gun."

I wasn't convinced, but Kemper had logic on his side. "I'm still reporting this. Forensics already knows about it. I'll just mention my observations. For all we know, it could connect to another case."

"Maybe that's why Lightman was so pissed off. Maybe the man we startled last night had nothing to do with the break-in. Maybe he hangs out in this alleyway and witnessed something much worse go down. That could be why he fled."

"Someone who lives in this alleyway wouldn't have a getaway car waiting."

"Maybe it wasn't a getaway car. Maybe it was his car. Y'know, just because a guy has a car, it doesn't mean he has to live in it."

"You think he was homeless?"

Kemper shrugged, making it up as he went along. "Possibly. Neither of us got a good look at him."

"Last night, you thought he was our suspect."

"I don't know, Lexie. That's what you said. That's what the paint indicated, but maybe we're wrong. Lightman wasn't convinced, which is why he sent us back here." Kemper headed for the mouth of the alley. "Come on. I'll buy you lunch."

I didn't want lunch. I wanted to know when a bullet went through the same dumpster where Kemper had been trapped. If our suspect had lured us into a trap, we were lucky to be alive.

Thoughts of my conversation with Michael this morning returned. My overprotective boyfriend had been concerned when he heard I was at the scene. Did he have a reason to worry? If so, I'd kill him for not telling me.

Kemper led us back to the shops and stores, where the streetlights could chase away the demons. "I'm in the mood for a gyro. Any objections?"

"No." My mind was elsewhere.

We stopped at a twenty-four hour Greek diner and ordered lunch. Well, it seemed like lunch to us. To the normal world, it would have seemed ridiculous. As we waited for our food, I stared out the window, noticing two men standing outside the sex shop across the street. The place closed an hour ago.

It was four a.m., and while it wasn't unusual to encounter people out and about, the men in dark clothing sent my radar buzzing. They looked like trouble.

I nudged Kemper, directing his attention to the suspicious looking men. "Maybe we should take a stroll while we wait for our order."

"Good idea."

Casually, we headed across the street. Although, it was hard for two uniformed police officers to appear casual at four in the morning. The men saw us coming and took to leaning against the brick wall. Based on their outfits and the backpacks slung over their shoulders, I couldn't help but wonder if they'd been involved in the jewelry store break-in.

The adult novelty shop would have a lot of cash on hand since most people didn't want charges like that to appear on their bank statements or credit card bills. According to the sign, the store wouldn't open again until ten a.m. The decal in the window said it was protected by Sunshine Security, the same alarm company from last night.

I narrowed my eyes at the men. Ink dripped over their collars and crept up their necks, but I couldn't make out enough of the tattoos to determine if they were members of a gang. They didn't wear colors or patches. They wore only black. As far as I could tell, there was no reason for them to be loitering outside this shop, at least no reason that was legal.

"Evening," Kemper greeted. "Can I help you gentlemen with anything?"

"Nah. We're good," the one on the left said.

"Right." Kemper looked from the store to the guy. "Would you mind showing me some identification?"

"What for?" the other guy asked. "We're not bothering anybody. It's not illegal to hang around or go for a walk."

His friend turned and gave him an angry glare, signaling he should shut up. "You don't need to see our IDs, officer. We aren't doing anything wrong." He cast his eyes upon me, staring far too long at my breasts. I was used to behavior like that when I was working undercover for vice, not while in full police uniform. "Don't you think you and the lady should get back to work and stop hassling us? You wouldn't want anything bad to happen behind your backs." He gave me a creepy, cold smile.

"I'm not a lady. I'm a cop." I pointed to my badge. "And the sign says no loitering. Kindly, move it along."

"Whatever. We're going," the other one said. "At least now we know when they'll be open." His eyes traveled up and down my body. "So we'll be back. Maybe we'll even get you something to play with."

"Do you want a citation for lewd behavior?" Kemper asked. "If not, I suggest you move it along."

"Sure thing." They took off down the street.

"Crisis averted," Kemper said as we went back to the diner to pick up our meals.

"At least for now." I kept my eyes on them and reached for my radio. I wasn't sure exactly what to call in, but I knew I should call this in.

SIX

"Sarconi, Kemper, get your asses in here," Lieutenant Peterson bellowed as soon as we set foot inside the station. Obediently, we went into his office. "You received a civilian complaint. Why were you harassing two men this morning?"

"Two men?" Kemper asked. "What two men?"

"You know which two," I mumbled before turning to Peterson. "We weren't harassing them. They looked suspicious. They were wearing dark clothing and loitering outside a closed shop at four in the morning. All we did was ask if they needed assistance."

"They didn't like the way you asked," Lt. Peterson said.

"I didn't like the way they answered."

"They're lucky we didn't issue a citation," Kemper said.

"What exactly did you do?" Peterson asked.

"I asked if I could see their IDs. They declined, and that was it."

"I heard you had another patrol unit follow them," Peterson said.

"We had reason to believe they may have been planning a break-in. In fact, I'm not convinced they weren't involved in the one at the jewelry store. That's why I notified Detective Lightman. He assigned someone to tail them. We were told to perform a canvass in the hopes of identifying any witnesses to that break-in," I said.

Lt. Peterson studied each of us for a moment, sighing loudly. "Fine, but don't let it happen again. In fact," Peterson looked at the roster, "I'm rescheduling the two of you. Things around here have been a little too hot lately, so take the next shift off. I don't want the idiots from internal affairs thinking I'm overlooking civilian complaints, even if they are bogus." He glowered at us. "This better be bogus."

"Yes, sir," I said.

Kemper muttered something under his breath and followed me to the locker rooms. "Can you believe this shit? We didn't do anything wrong. We might have even thwarted a crime-in-progress. But what thanks do we get? None. Instead, we get our wrists slapped and suspended for a day. This is bullshit." He kicked the locker room door. "This better not go on our records. We'll never pass the damn exam at this rate."

"We're not suspended. Suspensions look bad, and we would have been forced to sign something official. Think of this as a reward for our diligence." I wasn't an optimist by any stretch of the imagination, but this had very little to do with us and everything to do with what was going on at the station.

The lieutenant was feeling pressure from higher up, so he did his best to play politics without shafting us in the process. I wondered if any of it had to do with the bullet hole in the dumpster, but Kemper didn't want to consider the possibility. I had wanted to ask Lightman about it, but he had already left by the time we returned at the end of our shift.

"Some reward," Kemper griped as he headed out of the locker room. "It's an unpaid day off. It sucks no matter what spin you put on it."

After I changed back into my street clothes, I made a beeline for the exit. I wanted to call Michael. I had a lot of questions. Maybe, if I batted my eyelashes hard enough, he'd answer them.

I didn't even make it out the door before I spotted him parking his car in his usual space. Perfect timing.

"Hey, stranger," Michael greeted. "What are you still doing here?" He looked at his watch. "I know I'm running late, but you should have been home an hour ago."

"The lieutenant wanted to talk to us about a civilian complaint."

"Ouch. Are you okay? Do you want me to kick someone's ass?" Michael looked like he wanted to kiss me, but standing in the parking lot outside the station wasn't the place for that.

"That depends."

"On?"

I wanted to confront him, but now wasn't the time. He was late for work, and I needed to go home and think about things. "Never mind. It all worked out. I got a day off out of it."

"That's great." Michael studied my expression. "Not great?" His brow furrowed. "Peterson wouldn't suspend you."

"No, but being sidelined this close to the exam won't look good."

"Again, I'll ask if you want me to kick someone's ass."

"Yes, please," Kemper replied, interrupting us as he bounded down the steps. "Those two douchebags were casing that place. I don't care what anyone says. We confronted them, and they reconsidered committing the crime. Where does the lieutenant get off reprimanding us for that?"

"Kemper, let it go. It's a day off," I insisted. "This is why I told you initiative is bad. Head down. Remember?"

"They wouldn't have complained if they were innocent. They were seconds away from breaking into that shop. That's why they want to get us in hot water. We stopped them from getting paid. So they're returning the favor." Kemper shook his head. "This is unbelievable."

"I suggest you keep your protest to a minimum," Michael said, slipping into his formal police persona. "You'd hate to have that one day turn into two because you sound like an insubordinate rookie."

"C'mon, Riley," Kemper said, "I have every right to be pissed. It isn't fair. You were far more understanding when Sarconi was the one voicing the complaint. You wanted to kick someone's ass for her."

"She wasn't blaming the brass," Michael said.

"Whatever. I'll see you guys in a day or two. Have fun with that jewelry store thing."

Once Kemper was gone, Michael gave me a look. "Is he still being a jerk to you?"

"No."

"Really?" Michael didn't believe me.

"He's not the problem." I tried to move past, but he blocked my path.

"Are you mad at me?"

"No. Maybe. I don't know."

He lowered his voice. "Is this because I got called in the other morning?"

"No." I looked around, but we were alone, except for the security cameras. "Lightman sent Kemper and me back to the same neighborhood last night. He wanted us to find witnesses or evidence. Do you want to know what I found?"

Michael waited.

"A bullet hole in the dumpster."

"Forensics is analyzing it. Nothing's come back yet."

"Were you going to tell me?"

"We haven't spoken. When was I supposed to tell you about some random bullet that could have been there for months?"

"It wasn't."

Michael tilted his head in that defiant way. "How do you know that?"

"No rust around the hole. It couldn't have been made more than a week or two ago. But I'm guessing it was made two nights ago. That's why you were freaked out when I told you where I was. You knew."

"We'll talk about this later."

"You bet your ass we will."

"Oh, you want to bet my ass? How about I raise you?" Michael glanced around to make sure we were alone. "Meet me at my place at seven. I should be finished by then."

Despite my annoyance, it was hard to stay mad when he was being playful. So I decided to return the favor. "I'd like to be there when you finish."

"God, Lexie, you're killing me." His voice sounded hoarse. "Seven o'clock. If I'm not home when you get there, let yourself in. After we talk, we're gonna make the most out of your day off."

I went home, took a two hour nap, and forced myself out of bed at eleven a.m. It was important that I avoid sleeping the rest of the day. Since I was spending the night with Michael, I wanted to be on the same sleep schedule as him. Our evening together would be utterly pointless if I was passed out when he came home and he was unconscious by the time I woke up.

After brewing a pot of coffee, I decided the best way

to combat the fatigue would be to keep busy, so I spent the entire day reading the study guide and making flashcards. After completing the practice questions and rereading my notes, I felt more confident this was something I could do.

No more uniforms. No more patrols. No more civilians filing complaints over stupid shit. Smiling, I checked the time and hopped into the shower.

Thoughts of the graffiti painted on the jewelry store wall and those two tattooed men outside the sex shop played through my head. Kemper and I had been all over that neighborhood. We'd questioned every shop owner and civilian we came across. No one knew anything, or so they said. In fact, we hadn't spotted a single skull and crown painted on any walls or stores in the area. Why would the thief or thieves risk exposure by taking the time to paint that on the wall? Clearly, they wanted credit. So why didn't we know who they were?

Getting out of the shower, I went to my computer and performed an image search. But with thousands of potential hits, I didn't have the time or energy to sift through them all. Gangs knew what was going on. I just had to convince Michael to read me in. Normally, I wouldn't care this much, or so I tried to tell myself, but I knew what the hole in the dumpster meant. Someone took a shot at Kemper. I wanted to know who and why, especially if Lightman sent us back into that neighborhood a third time.

Slipping into my little black dress, I studied my reflection in the mirror. My long brown hair hung in loose waves, the way Michael liked it. The dress fit nicely, emphasizing my curves while making my waist and thighs look trim. Maybe it was a trick of the fabric or the physical demands of the job, but I looked nice for once, not the usual blah that happened after working too many long hours and wearing nothing but casual comfy clothes during my downtime.

Hopefully, I wasn't overdressed. We didn't have anything special planned, at least I didn't. I didn't know what Michael had in store, but I wanted answers. He said we'd talk. Maybe this would help convince him.

After packing an overnight bag, I made sure I had my key to Michael's place and headed for his apartment. When the clock on the dashboard clicked to seven, I stepped out of my car and made my way inside. I knocked on his apartment door, but there was no answer. I tried again, straining to hear sounds of the television or shower, but no noise emanated from within. He had been delayed.

When I pushed open the door, I thought he'd been burglarized. But nothing was missing or broken. The place had simply been hit by a mini tornado.

Michael must not have expected to work this late because he'd never invite me over when his place looked like this. He always straightened up first. Unless whatever he had to say was that important.

"Hello?" I called, checking each room. But his apartment was empty. No thieves, vandals, or Michael. Putting my bag down, I scanned the room. Where to begin? Dishes were piled in the sink. A basket of clean laundry waited to be folded.

Stepping out of my shoes, I poured myself a glass of wine from the open bottle in the fridge and put it down on the counter next to the sink. "You better appreciate me," I said, starting on the dishes.

Once they were washed, dried, and put away, I moved to the laundry basket. My last boyfriend had been a lying, cheating sack of shit, and it had become painfully obvious after finding his conquest's unmentionables in our laundry. So being an investigator by trade and neurotic by design, I sifted through Michael's laundry, finding nothing out of the ordinary.

He had t-shirts, jeans, socks, and boxer briefs, all of the male variety and all in his size. If he was stepping out on me, he was much smarter about it than Kevin had been, but considering that we were usually at work or asleep, Michael didn't have time to cheat, unless he was seeing someone at work, and that didn't seem likely since I also worked there. Plus, I doubted he'd do that to me, particularly after my best friend, Amber, threatened to hurt him if he so much as looked at another woman. Yeah, Amber could be a handful. It was a good thing she was a hospital administrator and not a cop, or people would end up dead.

Snooping wasn't exactly the best idea, but Michael should have known better than to leave me unsupervised in his apartment. Now that the place was tidy and somewhat livable, I looked through his kitchen cabinets, scanned his movie collection, checked the products in his medicine cabinet, and stumbled upon a case file sitting atop his desk. Even if it was my night off, I couldn't help but wonder what was so important that he'd break his rule about bringing work home with him.

I opened the folder, not surprised to find a photo of the skull and crown paperclipped to the inside cover. This was a big case. It's why Lightman showed up minutes after Kemper and I responded to the call. And as I flipped the pages, I realized why Michael had been so concerned when he learned I was at the scene.

SEVEN

The smash and grab at the jewelry store was the fourth break-in in the last two weeks. Stills taken from surveillance footage showed two masked men entering four different shops, including the jewelry store. The men wore all black and carried backpacks, just like the two guys Kemper and I had questioned last night. Unlike the men we spoke to, the criminals in these photos wore gas masks and left their calling card stenciled on the wall of every place they hit.

None of the shops showed signs of forced entry, but display cases and cash drawers had been smashed or pried open. Whoever did this had no problem gaining entry, even though they set off the alarms at every location. However, that didn't deter them from breaking things, and they never appeared in a hurry to leave. Every single graffiti tag they left was completed and colored. They didn't seem worried about getting caught, or they knew exactly how long it'd take the police to arrive. And they had no qualms about destroying everything and anything once they were inside the shops. It was just the outside they kept pristine.

From the case file and Michael's notes, the gangs unit had taken the case over from grand larceny as soon as word of the tagging reached them. Only one gang used that tag to mark their territory—the Skulls. A month ago, one of their upper echelon had been killed by police officers executing a raid. Several other members of the gang had been arrested and were currently being held.

The death of one of their own had led to rumblings. The Skulls were out for revenge. The more cops they killed, the better.

No one at the station had mentioned this. Patrol hadn't been briefed or warned about the situation. The brass had swept it under the rug. The official assessment determined the threat wasn't credible.

I scanned the copy of the report, not believing a word of it. The bullet hole in the dumpster indicated otherwise. The paint splotches placed in that alleyway and the strategic way the tarp had been hung told me my assumptions had been correct. Kemper and I had walked into a trap. What didn't make sense is how we walked out alive.

I read Michael's notes, finding comfort in that familiar crooked scrawl. Gangs was investigating every instance and reevaluating the potential threat, but the Skulls weren't that big of an organization. They didn't control enough territory, leading to the theory the thieves were intentionally using that gang symbol to throw us off their scent.

I wasn't sure I bought it, particularly with what I'd learned in the last twenty-four hours. The way Michael reacted that morning in my bedroom told me he wasn't convinced either. That's why forensics was analyzing the bullet in the alleyway. If the Skulls were behind the jewelry store break-in, their goal wasn't just to make off with the loot. They were out for blood. My blood. Kemper's blood. Any blood that ran blue.

I thought about the latest scene. Kemper and I

hadn't gotten to review the security footage in any real detail, but from Michael's notes, a third man on the crew provided technical support to bypass the exterior security systems. My gut said this unknown third man worked for Sunshine Security since all the targeted locations were under their protection. Did the Skulls have one of their own inside the security company?

Flipping through the pages, I didn't see any transcripts or logs indicating Sunshine Security had been contacted, nor did I find a list of potential future targets. Granted, that information could be in an official folder inside the station and not sitting on Michael's desk at home, but it was the most likely avenue to explore. I pulled a sticky note from the dispenser and wrote down my theory, leaving it next to the folder. Michael didn't like to talk about work outside of work since he felt it was a waste of our time together, but he would find my note eventually. If he thought my hints were foolish or sophomoric, I wouldn't be around to see him crumple up the note and toss it away.

Now that I was through reading the case file, I had nothing else to do. I should have brought my study guide. Instead, I flipped channels for a while.

As the hours ticked by, the fatigue set in. Why wasn't Michael home yet? Why hadn't he called? I tried texting, but he didn't respond.

The case file on his desk only ratcheted up my concern. Gangs was going after the Skulls, and the Skulls were going after cops. And Michael wasn't home. Maybe I should go to the station. I could always pretend I forgot something in my locker. But I was already on thin ice with Lt. Peterson. And assuming the worst was premature.

More than likely, Michael had gotten stuck working overtime. I just as easily could have been delayed by a work snafu. It was the job, but it was a dangerous job. I swallowed, hoping Michael was okay. *It would be stupid to worry*, I told myself, feeling the unease settle in the pit of my stomach.

The dress was starting to get uncomfortable, so I dug through the pile of clean laundry. Slipping into his t-shirt, which fit like a dress, I sprawled out on the couch. I'd rather have him delayed than hurt.

The fact that he wasn't home yet and hadn't called wasn't necessarily cause for alarm, but we didn't have the best track record. Anything could have happened. He could have gotten held up with a last minute call. That must be it. It happened all the time. I turned the television back on, hoping to distract myself from worrying.

When I couldn't silence the negative thoughts, I poured another glass of wine. He was okay. Everything was okay.

Normally, I didn't worry. But he said he'd be finished by seven, and it was now 11:30. He was four and a half hours late.

Maybe he went to my place instead, or Detective Lightman made him work late. Michael was fine. I repeated this a few times while I finished my wine. Putting the glass down, I took a deep, calming breath. The wine didn't do much to relax me, so I got up and settled in at his desk. If Michael was going to work late, the least I could do was help.

EIGHT

The front door slammed, and I practically jumped out of my skin and scrambled for my gun. I drew on the intruder, my finger resting on the trigger guard. Michael Riley raised both hands and took a step back.

"Easy, Lex. It's only me." He smiled. "I know I'm late, but are you really angry enough to shoot me?"

Putting the gun down, I ran a hand over my face and eased back in the chair, clutching my chest dramatically. "Jesus, Michael. You know better than to scare me like that."

He knelt on the floor next to me, burying his face in my neck. "Honey, I'm so sorry. I got here as soon as I could. Things were crazy tonight. I wanted to call, but I never found the time to do it." He pulled away from the embrace and kissed me. "You look exhausted."

"Thanks, that's just what a girl likes to hear. What happened at work?"

He shook his head and stood, taking off his jacket and emptying his pockets. "I'll tell you about it in the morning. Let's get you to bed." He scooped me into his arms and carried me to the bedroom. "I see you found my pile of laundry."

"You said we would talk when you got home. I read the case file. Gangs thinks the Skulls are gunning for cops."

"It's just a theory." Michael unbuttoned his shirt as he went into the bathroom. A few seconds later, the water turned on.

"A theory? Some asshole set a trap and took a shot at Kemper."

"We don't know that yet."

Getting up, I moved closer to the bathroom door, finding my limbs heavy and sluggish. I needed to sleep, but this was more important. "Did forensics determine anything about the bullet?"

"It was badly damaged. Ballistics is still working on it." He poked his head out of the shower to look at me. "Jack said you only saw one guy in that alleyway."

"I saw one guy fleeing the scene. I didn't get a good look at anyone in the alley before the asshole tossed the tarp over me."

"What about the gunshot? Neither you nor Kemper made any mention of it in your reports."

"We heard a bang. We couldn't identify the source. Maybe the acoustics were off."

"C'mon, Lex, we all know damn well what gunfire sounds like." The look on his face told me he wanted it to be true. He wanted me to be blowing this out of proportion, but the look in his eyes said he knew better.

"What if he had a homemade silencer or suppressor? It'd sound different. And with Kemper banging around inside the dumpster, it could have confused things."

Michael finished showering, grabbed a towel, wrapped it around his waist, and pulled open the shower curtain. "If the Skulls were hoping to exact revenge, they wouldn't have sent one guy. They don't operate alone. They're like dogs. They travel in packs."

"You ever hear of a lone wolf?"

He swallowed, moving past me and into the bedroom. He pulled on a pair of pajama pants beneath his towel before removing it from his waist and drying his chest. The water droplets clung to his defined pecs, but I was too stressed and aggravated to allow that to distract me. Then he ran the towel through his hair, making it stick out in every direction. "I don't want to say it, Lexie. I don't want to put it out there."

"But you think if Kemper and I had gone up against the Skulls that we'd both be dead now."

Michael shrugged, looking away. "You would have been an easy target."

The words stung, like I had screwed up. But Michael didn't say it to be mean. I was too tired not to get emotional over this, especially after getting chewed out this morning because of the same men I believed were responsible.

"Do they have tattoos?" I asked, hoping to hide my trembling chin.

"Who?"

"The Skulls."

"A lot of gangs have ink. But they don't have a specific symbol or mark. They aren't Rangers or SEALs. We can't identify their members that way."

"But they use that skull and crown symbol to mark their territory."

"Lexie, it's late. We'll discuss this in the morning."

"What were you doing all night?"

"Like I said, Jack and I were trying to figure out what's what."

"And you couldn't take two seconds to reply to my text?"

Michael ran a hand down his hair. "I didn't have my phone."

"Why not?"

He sighed, knowing I wouldn't give this up. "We went to the prison to speak to the men we have incarcerated. We were there until lights out. I didn't get my phone back until we left, and the battery was dead. By the time it was charged, I thought it'd be too late to reply, so I came home instead."

I fought to keep my eyes open and my legs from giving out.

Michael reached for me and pulled me toward the bed. "We'll talk more in the morning. Neither of us is thinking clearly right now. If we keep this up, we're bound to fight, and I don't want that. I've barely seen you in weeks."

I snuggled against Michael. "Work's killing us. How are we supposed to make it when we never see one another?"

"It won't be like this forever."

"I should probably tell you while I was waiting for you to get home, I finished your wine and snooped through every inch of your apartment because I'm a little crazy, and I was going stir crazy."

"I'm just glad you didn't run for the hills when you found out what a slob I am."

"You're a slob? You mean someone didn't break in and trash the place?"

His hand snuck inside my shirt and darted across my stomach so he could tickle me. I squirmed against him while he laughed and nibbled on my earlobe. "Don't be mad," he finally said.

"I'm not. I just want to know what's going on."

"Tomorrow," he murmured. "I promise."

When I woke up from a dreamless sleep at three a.m., the only thing I recalled was peace and darkness. It was a nice reprieve, one of those sound sleeps that made me feel like a new person, even if I'd only been out cold for a little over an hour.

Michael was wrapped around me, treating my body like a child would a teddy bear. One of his legs was thrown over mine, and his arm was wrapped possessively around my waist. Wiggling out of his grasp, I went into the kitchen to get a glass of water.

The bright glare from the overhead light was harsh on my eyes, and I squinted at my reflection in the stainless steel toaster. At least I wasn't out on patrol.

Maybe the lateness of the hour was impairing my judgment, but I found my purse on the table, dug out my phone, and called in sick for the following shift. Then I went back to bed, placed my head on Michael's shoulder, and wished our night had gone as planned.

My dreams were typically one of two varieties, nightmares or humdrum, nonsensical events. That wasn't true this morning. This time, I dreamt Michael and I were making out inside the locker room. Someone entered, so Michael pulled us into one of the shower stalls, barely managing to get the curtain closed before we were discovered. But that didn't stop him from taking our making out from PG-13 to NC-17. I bit my lip to keep from crying out.

If the brass knew what we were up to, we'd both be unemployed. Yet a part of me wanted to scream in ecstasy to set us free from the invisible shackles work had placed upon our relationship.

The sound of my own whimpers and moans woke me. Opening my eyes, I realized it was morning. I was lying on Michael's chest. We weren't at work. More importantly, he wasn't at work.

"What are you doing here?" I asked, seeing an amused smirk light up his face.

"I'm enjoying listening to you." He exhaled, his eyes closing briefly. "Tell me you were dreaming about me."

My leg was draped across his torso. He held it in

place with a firm hand on my thigh while his other hand rubbed my back. He was clearly turned on, and I flushed crimson.

"This is so embarrassing." I lifted my head off his chest. "Why didn't you wake me?"

"I was curious to see what would happen," he said slyly. My cheeks continued to heat at his words. "As far as I know, this is the most action either of us has seen in two weeks." His hand moved to my waist. "Were you dreaming about me?"

I nodded.

"Good."

"Why aren't you at work?" I asked.

"Jack told me to take the day." He kissed my forehead. "I'm sorry about last night."

"And I'm sorry about unconsciously molesting you."

"You can molest me anytime you want." He flipped us over and pinned me against the mattress. "I found the entire thing incredibly erotic." His erection pressed into my stomach, and in my already turned on state, an expectant moan escaped from the depths of my throat. "Lexie, I really am sorry about last night. Like I said, I wanted to call, but there just wasn't time."

"This isn't working."

"I know." He gave me a gentle kiss. "I'm working and then you're working, so we can't work together. How many days until the detective's exam?"

"Nineteen." I sighed. "Do you think it'll even matter? There's no guarantee I'll pass, and even if I do, we could still be working opposite shifts. I hope that won't happen, but it could."

"Maybe you should take Jack up on his offer. You could work for gangs. We could work together."

"Preston would love that."

"Samantha?" Michael gave me that look which meant he didn't want to talk about his ex. "She wouldn't care."

"Do you even think we could work together? We'd have to disclose. The brass could decide to keep us apart."

"It's only a problem if we're in the same chain of command. If we're both gangs detectives, I wouldn't be bossing you around. The only one who bosses us around is Jack, and that's because he's in charge of the unit."

"Which I still don't understand when he's a detective like the rest of you."

"Haven't you ever noticed his badge?" Michael asked. "He made sergeant, but he hates the designation. He wants people to know he's leading the investigation. That's why he insists on remaining 'Detective'."

"Sounds like Lightman."

"C'mon, Lex. What do you say? We can't be nothing more than ships passing in the night. I care too much about you to let this fizzle. I don't want that." He peppered my neck and collarbone with open-mouthed kisses. "You don't want that either. What's holding you back? Don't you want me? Don't you want to be with me every chance you get, like your dream would suggest?" He stopped kissing me long enough to press his palm against my chest, feeling my heart race. "I'd say your body's saying yes. I think you should listen to it."

"You know I can't say no to you." I narrowed my eyes at him. "But we shouldn't work together. We'll figure something else out. The problem is I'm working graveyard and you're working days. That could happen even if we both work for gangs. Shifts change. We all have to serve our time. The only way to fix that is to get on the same rotation, and that's never a guarantee."

"It is if we're partners."

"We can't work together."

"Because we're sleeping together?"

"Because you would kill anyone who tried to hurt me."

"Nonsense. I'd respond with the appropriate amount of force."

"You shot the last guy who attacked me."

Michael sighed dramatically. "He would have killed you if he got the chance. I made sure that didn't happen."

"I can take care of myself."

"I know that."

I grasped his face and forced him to look me in the eye. "Do you?"

"Yes, Lexie. We've been over this." He reached for the hem of my shirt and grasped the edges. "But that doesn't mean I won't have your back, just like I expect you to have mine. And I won't apologize for doing whatever I have to in order to protect you or any other cop in trouble. That's the code. We have each other's backs."

"Even Kemper's?"

"That depends. You've been riding with him these last few weeks. Has he tried to make a move on you?"

"Did you miss the part where I said I could take care of myself?"

Michael tugged on my t-shirt. "How about we stop talking about this and we take care of each other?" He lowered his head and whispered in my ear. "Let's pick up where your dream left off."

NINE

Sated, Michael collapsed on top of me, and I clung to him. As he rolled us over, so not to crush me, I realized this was all I wanted. We had to find a way to make it work. To make our schedules work. Snuggling against him, I felt myself drifting in and out while our breathing and heart rates returned to normal.

Finally, I found my voice. "I called in sick."

"How'd you know I was getting off today?"

"I only wear uncomfortable underwear and my little black dress for one reason."

He laughed. "I will keep that in mind for future reference."

I rested my chin against his chest so I could look into his eyes. "In all seriousness, I needed a break from work. I miss you, and it's making me hate the job, especially with whatever is going on at that damn jewelry store."

"Are you getting burnt out?" His hands ran through my hair, untangling the mess it always became after sleep or sex. In this case, both. "Or is it from having to patrol every night with that whiny jerk?"

"Kemper?"

"What other whiny jerks do you know?"

"He's my partner. Sure, he can be an ass, but he's

okay most of the time." I paused to collect my thoughts. "These night patrols are tedious and sometimes a little scary. The dark makes it difficult to determine what you're rolling up on. Last night, when you were running late, my mind came up with a lot of unsettling scenarios. Were you really at the prison all night?"

His hands grasped my face, and he kissed me. "Until lights out. After that, Jack received word of another smash and grab. This one turned violent. The responding officer was attacked."

"Jesus." I sat up, pulling the sheet around me. "Who was hurt?"

"Officer Daniel Cruise." Michael studied me. "Do you know him?"

I shook my head.

"He didn't get a good look at his attacker, but I'm sure it's the same team we've been chasing."

"The Skulls?"

"We're still deciding that, but I'd say it's the same team who broke into the jewelry store and three other shops." Michael scratched his eyebrow. "You read the file. You know almost as much as I do."

"How do you not know if the Skulls are behind this? The tag on the wall says they are. I'd think Cruise getting attacked would further support that conclusion."

"Like the bullet hole in the dumpster?" Michael asked.

"Exactly."

He licked his lips, unsure if he should say what was on his mind. "Lex, think about it. The Skulls made it clear they want to see as many cops dead as possible, but they haven't acted openly on that threat. If members of that gang are behind these break-ins, they wouldn't have just hurt Cruise. They would have killed him." He swallowed. "And Kemper."

"And me."

"Don't put that out there."

"But that's what you were thinking."

"I don't know what to think."

"You said we were going to talk about this. Tell me what you're thinking."

"I think I don't want you anywhere near that neighborhood. I hate that you were the one who responded to the alarm. Jack wants you and Kemper to continue to poke around and ask questions. I don't like it, and I told him as much." He held up his hand before I could protest. "This isn't because I want to keep you safe, even though I do. It's because any uniformed officers we send in to ask questions will serve no other purpose than to antagonize the Skulls. They're already itching for a fight. I'd rather we deescalate the situation."

"What did Lightman say?"

"He wants to stop them before this turns into all-out warfare. The only way he thinks that will happen is if we arrest the party responsible, regardless of who they are or their gang affiliations."

"Makes sense."

"Maybe. Maybe not. Of course, it doesn't help that Sunshine Security, the company who installed the systems at every single crime scene, hires reformed criminals to ensure the efficacy of their product. The man in charge of those checks, Adan Shaw, was the Skulls' original founder. He got out of the life after serving a nickel. Now, he claims he's an upstanding member of society. He got cherry-picked by the security company as the poster boy for felons turned friends."

"Felons turned friends?"

"Whatever you want to call it. That program that

places ex-cons with jobs that require the skills they used for their illegal ventures. Don't get me wrong. I've seen guys turn over a new leaf, but it's rare. Even when it does happen, family ties can get in the way. Since Shaw put the gang on the map as a bunch of tough shits who take what they want and his little brother's the only one left standing to run the current regime, I can't help but think the break-ins and the gang are connected."

"You think that's why those shops were targeted? They were easy marks. Shaw gave them keys or whatever they needed to gain entry to the buildings."

"Maybe."

"Why didn't he tell them how to turn off the alarm?" That's why the brass had called the jewelry store break-in a heist. It looked like Kemper was right. There was an inside man. It all made sense now.

"We have several theories."

"One being the Skulls want to lure cops to the locations and kill them."

"Another being whoever is responsible wants to make sure we're convinced the Skulls are responsible."

"Evidence backs that."

"Except for the graffiti, the rest is circumstantial. And frankly, anyone can use a stencil and spray paint to create the symbol on the wall." Michael sat up beside me, letting his fingers wander up my neck before kissing me again. He hoped to distract me from the shoptalk.

"If the Skulls aren't behind this, who do you think is?"

"Anyone," he said between kisses. "Rival gangs. Thieves."

"What do you think they're after?"

"A big score."

"How big?"

Michael gave up on trying to distract me with kisses. "I thought you didn't want to work together." He moved in front of me, pinning me against the headboard and shifting his hips which made my breath catch. "Have you changed your mind?" He rocked against me. "This isn't your case, Lex. You don't have to waste your time on it."

"What if I changed my mind?"

"Was it something I said?" He grinned like a Cheshire cat. "Or something I did?"

"You don't play fair."

"I think we should be partners. Jack already thinks you want in on this case. I could say you approached me about it and suggest he pair us together again."

"He didn't like us working together last time. He thought we were distracted." I fought not to let what Michael's hips were doing prove Lightman's point.

"He may not have liked it, but we got results. If we do it again, I bet that'd secure your spot on the team and as my partner once you trade your badge for that bright, shiny detective's shield in a few weeks."

"Fine, but Kemper wants in too."

"Jack made you the offer, not him."

"Yes, but Peterson has us riding together. I'm guessing that means we're a package deal."

"I could offer you a different package deal."

My eyes went wide, and I lightly slapped his arm. "Michael."

"What? You're naked in my bed with sex hair. I can't help it."

"Answer my question first. Do you honestly believe we're capable of working together without this," I gestured to the area around us, "getting in the way?"

"It's Jack's decision. He's in charge. But I won't jump your bones while on a stakeout, if that's what you're worried about."

It wasn't, and he knew it. I didn't know what I should say or do. The thought of working on another investigation with him was alluring. It wasn't even my idea. Kemper wanted this. Now that civilians were filing complaints, I worried what would happen between now and the exam. The last thing I needed was to have to explain myself to the review board. Until now, my record was practically spotless. Sure, the johns accused me of entrapment, but those complaints fell on deaf ears. We had recordings to prove otherwise.

"Fine, but make sure you say Kemper and I both want in. Lightman can decide who he wants to take, and he won't think you're giving me preferential treatment."

"Okay. Tomorrow, I'll talk to Jack about getting you off patrol and back to assisting us on the investigation." Michael smiled. "Now let's get back to other things."

We remained in bed for another hour, cuddling, talking, and getting reacquainted. I missed him, and spending the morning wrapped in his arms was exactly what I needed. Unfortunately, my bladder eventually demanded that I get out of our cozy, euphoric bed.

I picked his t-shirt up off the floor and put it on before making the trek to the bathroom. After relieving myself, brushing my teeth, and taming my knotted hair, I returned to the bedroom and settled back against his chest. He brushed a lock of my hair from my face and smiled.

"Am I forgiven?" he asked.

"For what?"

"Coming home late. Failing to call. Worrying you."

"I told you I was never mad at you." I traced my

finger along the ridges of his torso, making his muscles tense and jump. Michael Riley was ticklish. That was something I'd have to remember.

"Regardless, I want to make it up to you. Since we have today off, let's do something fun."

"We've already had fun. Lots of fun."

He kissed my shoulder. "I'm glad you enjoyed yourself. I know I did. If you play your cards right, we'll have more fun tonight."

"Someone's talking a big game. Are you sure you're up for it? I'd hate to be disappointed."

"Have I ever disappointed you in bed?" he asked, sounding genuinely concerned.

"No. In fact, it's the only reason I put up with your ridiculous job and work schedule. I mean, who in their right mind would date a cop?"

"Clearly, a lunatic," he said, playing along. "So what do you want to do today? Anything you want, just name it."

"Michael, seriously, it's fine. This is enough."

He cocked an eyebrow up questioningly. "If you could do anything, what would it be?"

"I don't know. Why are you asking that? What's going on?" My stomach clenched, fearing the other shoe was about to drop.

"Nothing, but if you want to celebrate our three month anniversary, we should do it today."

"We haven't been dating three months yet. That's at the end of next week."

It wasn't much of a milestone. Technically, an anniversary required a year, but we missed doing something special to celebrate our first month together because it took us that long to figure out when we started dating. Two false starts had a little something to do with it, and we had been too busy to remember when the two month mark hit. So he insisted we should do something spectacular if we made it to three.

"You're the one who wanted to celebrate. Why are we throwing something together today?" I asked. He looked guilty, and I scrutinized him. "You aren't going to be around next week."

He ran a hand through his hair. "I would love to take you somewhere and do the whole rose petals, champagne, and chocolates thing, but," he got off the bed and went to the drawer, momentarily distracting me with his gorgeous body, "the lieutenant posted the schedules for next week, and I'm working. Assuming we haven't stopped these jewel thieves by then, it'll be another week of long hours and lots of overtime. I'm just being realistic. We have the time now. We should make the most of it."

"Did you seriously call them jewel thieves? That's very international man of mystery. Are you a spy?"

"They do get laid a lot." He considered the idea while grabbing clean clothes from his dresser. "Would you date a spy?"

"Absolutely not. It'd be nothing but lies and deceit, and you know I have trust issues."

"Does that mean you were serious when you said you searched my apartment while I was at work?"

"Yeah."

He snorted and disappeared into the bathroom. "I should have known."

"Hey, at least I admitted it." Finding my overnight bag that contained a change of clothes, more practical underwear, and my toiletries, I retrieved my dress from the kitchen chair and went into the bathroom.

TEN

Michael had already showered and was shaving when I entered. Pulling off the shirt I wore, I flashed him before stepping into the shower. If he wanted to go somewhere fancy, I wasn't going to rain on his parade. Honestly, I couldn't remember the last time we went out. Surely, that wasn't normal for a couple who'd been dating less than three months.

Once we were both dressed, we left his apartment with no real destination in mind. We were right in the middle of brunch when Michael's cell phone rang. He growled, dropping his fork and reaching into his pocket.

"It's Jack."

"You should answer it." I skewered a strawberry off the top of his pancakes.

"Riley," he said, leaning back in the chair. "Uh-huh. Sure." He paused, listening to whatever Lightman had to say. "Okay, I can do that. I'll let you know what I find."

"That doesn't sound good." I checked the time. At least we'd gotten to spend the entire morning and the early afternoon together.

"New plan." Michael knocked my fork away before I could snatch a slice of banana off his plate. "First, you're getting your own order of strawberry banana pancakes. Then we'll finish our leisurely brunch and run an errand for Jack. It shouldn't take too long. We have reservations at seven, and we're not missing them, even if it means walking out in the middle of a follow-up interview."

"You're taking me along to work the case?"

"It won't hurt since you're already up to speed on everything. It's as if you read the entire case file last night." He gave me a pointed look.

"It was out in the open, begging me to pick it up."

Michael chuckled. "I know. I found your sticky note when you were in the shower. I reached the same conclusion you did."

"Adan Shaw," I said.

"Yes, but you didn't know anything about him until this morning when I filled you in when we just so happened to run into each other." He pointed the tines of his fork at me. "Make sure you remember that if Jack asks."

"I'll remember."

"Good." Michael smiled. "Those are detective chops you've got there, Lexie."

"It's called common sense, Michael. Anyone could have deduced that."

"You need to learn how to take a compliment." He used his fork to cut off a wedge of pancake and stuffed it in his mouth. "Everything points to Shaw assisting the thieves, but we have no proof yet. Jack wants someone to check with the jewelry store owner to see if he recalled the technician's name who installed the system. When we spoke to him a few nights ago, he said the work order was elsewhere, but he never got back to us."

"He might recognize me. I was at the scene the night it happened."

"So?"

"I called in sick today. I'm wearing a dress, and I'm out with you. Don't you think Lightman's going to realize what's going on?"

"Only if you tell him. If not, he won't care. Trust me. Department relationships aren't high on his list of priorities."

"You'd know."

Michael met my eyes. "Yes, I would." He cracked a smile, letting me know he had no desire to fight or rehash the details of his previous relationship. "Oh, I see what the actual problem is now. You're afraid the jewelry store owner will take one look at you and realize what we were doing this morning."

"Michael." I blushed.

"We're following up with the store owner. He isn't going to give it a second thought either, and it's not like Jack has the place staked out to see if I show up to an active crime scene with a date."

"Okay, but if I have to write a report, we better have our stories straight. I don't want this to bite me in the ass. I can't afford that right now."

"I know. I'd never jeopardize your career or your safety. Do you trust me, Lex?"

"Yes."

"Maybe tell your face that." He called the waitress over and ordered a stack of pancakes for me.

After brunch, which consisted of my omelet and eating the strawberries and bananas off the pancakes and watching Michael finish the rest, we headed to the jewelry store. In the light of day, it looked a lot different. The storefront was all glass and shiny black metal. None of the doors or windows had been damaged. The only damage sustained was to the large central display case.

Despite the official police tape that covered the

door to deter entry, there were no obvious signs of what occurred. The yellow tape had been sliced at the seam by whoever had entered. Michael pushed the door open. Inside, the store appeared empty.

"Police," he announced. "Is anyone here?"

"Just a second," a male voice called from the back.

While we waited, I surveyed the room. Evidence collection was completed. The security footage was taken to the station, along with whatever evidence the crime scene techs found. The rest of the room had been dusted for prints. Bits of black powder remained on a few surfaces from where it had dripped off the brush.

"Can I help you?" Mr. Cline, the store owner, asked. He emerged from the back hallway and gave me the quick once-over. "We're closed, miss."

"I know." I reached into my purse for my badge.

Michael interrupted, holding out his detective's shield. "Mr. Cline, maybe you remember us. I'm Detective Riley. This is Officer Sarconi. Detective Lightman said you'd be here."

"Right. Right." Cline nodded to himself and went to the cash register in the far corner of the room. "I found that work order from the security system in my files at home." He held it up but refused to hand it over. "I'll make a copy for you, Detective. I need the original for my insurance."

"While you do that, can I see what the back looks like?" Michael asked.

"Help yourself." Cline headed toward the office in the rear.

Michael leaned closer to me. "I'll be right back. Look around. Let me know if we missed anything."

I walked the perimeter. Two of the walls were nothing more than large, picturesque windows. Despite the dark tinting, they provided a panoramic view of the city. Thin microfilaments were etched into the glass, designed to detect a break or breach.

The control panel to turn off the security system was on the wall closest to the front door. From my initial walkthrough, I remembered seeing an identical panel in the back, near the rear exit. Following the cables, I determined one of them went to the monitor near the cashier's desk and the other disappeared into the ceiling tiles.

The front door had a sliding metal gate that covered the glass and had to be manually unlocked. But the gate had been open the night I responded to the call. The actual door had a keypad that would only disengage the lock when the correct six digit number was entered or a key was inserted. I couldn't determine if entry required both a number and a key or one or the other.

If it only required a key, the door could have been jimmied open which would undermine the security system and put a chink in our theory that the thieves were tipped off by someone inside Sunshine Security on how to bypass the system. But I never spotted any tool marks. Even now, it didn't look like the lock had been compromised.

My gut said the thieves knew the code. We just had to prove it. I wondered if the security footage showed anything.

Heading around back, I listened to my heels echo in the enclosed alleyway. On the bright side, it was unlikely someone would be able to sneak up behind me without being heard. The rear door had a similar keypad and locking mechanism. But this door hadn't been breached either.

On my way back to the front, I noticed my reflection in the store windows. The glass didn't allow outsiders to see in. Instead, it reflected a mirror image of the surrounding street. At night, it'd be easier to see inside the store, but the best view required cupping one's hands around one's face and pressing against the window.

"Riley," I called, opening the door, "were the exterior windows checked for evidence?"

"Why would we need to check the windows?" Mr. Cline asked, stepping out of the office with Michael at his heels. "They weren't broken and obviously weren't used to get inside."

"What are you thinking, Sarconi?" Michael's brow furrowed. He tilted his head to the side to study the nearest window.

"If our thieves were smart, they might have tried to get a peek inside to make sure the place was empty before breaking in."

"And if they were stupid, they didn't bother to wipe the glass afterward." Michael smiled. "And you wondered why I wanted you to tag along."

ELEVEN

After phoning the station to find out how thorough the crime scene investigators had been, Michael checked the time. According to him, we were right on schedule. While he drove to our next destination which he was keeping secret, I asked if anything had been discovered concerning my new hunch.

The windows had been examined for signs of damage, but considering the amount of foot traffic that went past the store on a daily basis, the techs opted not to waste their time printing the windows since the thieves wore gloves.

"It was worth a shot," Michael said. He handed me the copy of the work order. "Just like thinking Adan Shaw was our inside man. But according to this, Shaw didn't work on the security system. We'll have to dig through Sunshine's records, but what we thought would be rock-solid proof is now nothing more than unsubstantiated speculation."

"Are the other crime scenes similar to this one? The layout, not the actual robbery. Obviously, those are similar, or you wouldn't be working under the assumption it's the same crew."

"You mean those details weren't in the files you read last night?" He feigned shock.

"I must have missed them."

"I thought you read every word."

"I did."

"And you don't remember?"

I knew he was teasing me, but I didn't like it. "I was preoccupied with washing dishes and folding your laundry."

"If I'd gotten home in time, I would have cleaned up. You didn't have to do housework. That's not why I asked you over."

"I know, but I thought I'd help out."

"I warned you my apartment is rarely ready for company."

"At least your closet, cabinets, and drawers are organized. I almost feared getting buried beneath an avalanche when I opened your coat closet."

"Maybe you shouldn't have searched my whole place."

I couldn't tell if he was amused or mad. "I plead the fifth."

"Dammit, Lexie. I thought you said you trusted me."

"I do. I just got bored, and your laundry was asking to be searched for slutty thongs."

"Phew." He wiped his forehead with the back of his hand. "It's a good thing Bambi came by to pick up her stripper outfit two days ago."

"I know that's a joke made at my expense, but it's not funny."

He turned, seeing the intense hurt in my eyes. "I'm sorry. You know I'm not a cheater. You know how deplorable I find it. We've both experienced it firsthand. But I've spent almost every night at your place. What did you think you would find?"

"I don't know."

"That's why I'm not sure you trust me. Instead of

realizing you wouldn't find anything, you didn't know what you'd find." He pressed his lips together and shook his head. "Search as much as you want if that's what it'll take for you to learn to relax around me. But I hope one of these days you'll realize I won't do anything to hurt you."

"So the layout of the other break-ins?" I asked, wondering if all of that was meant to distract me.

"The shops were all a little different, but they shared several common traits. Metal bars over the doors. The same security system. That's about it. The thieves never explored any farther than the main showroom. As far as we know, they never wasted time breaking into any offices or safes."

"Smash and grabs with a side of vandalism."

"Basically."

The rest of our ride was in silence. Talking about this frustrated Michael. Part of the reason he was annoyed was because work ruined our night and had taken up part of our day together. He had yet to admit we couldn't separate it from the rest of our lives. It wasn't who we were, and it wasn't what this job allowed.

"We're here." He pulled into the valet line. "No more shoptalk, deal?"

"Deal." I looked out the window. "Are you sure we're in the right place?" We were outside one of the finest galleries in the city.

"Yep." He reached into the back seat, grabbed a garment bag, unzipped it, and removed his jacket. "I didn't want to be too dressed up in front of Mr. Cline. We wouldn't have wanted him to get the wrong idea." He shrugged into his jacket, flipped down the vanity mirror, and adjusted his tie.

"You just mentioned something related to work. See, it's not as easy as you make it sound."

"Fine. We'll keep count of who slips up the most. Tonight, the loser pays. We're having dinner across the street."

I turned to see the fancy French restaurant. "I don't think I can afford that place. Frankly, I don't think you can either."

"That's not what I meant." He winked.

The valet opened my door, and I stepped out, waiting for Michael to come around the car and meet me. He put an arm around my waist and whispered something very inappropriate in my ear. I gaped at his highly explicit suggestion.

"Fine, but I hope you're prepared to put your money where your mouth is," I retorted, letting him guide us inside, "because a lady would never do that."

"It's a good thing I'm not a lady," he said.

~*~

"Did you have fun today?" he asked. It was almost midnight, and we had just gotten into bed.

"Yes." A million-watt smile erupted on my face. "How did you get a reservation at that restaurant, let alone a private tour of the art gallery across the street?"

"One of the artists is a close friend of mine. Since his pieces are on display right now, he gets to make the guest list, so he put me on it."

"You have friends who are artists?"

Michael smiled. "There's a lot you don't know about me."

I settled against the pillow and stared at him. "You make everything look so easy. The job mostly. Although, I never expected Detective Ruggedly Handsome to be such a sweet guy. You put together the perfect date with no prep or planning. It was amazing."

"Should I be insulted?"

"That was a compliment."

"But sweet?" He made a face. "Me? What would the people at work think about that?"

I poked him, making him smile. "Relax. You're a badass. You wear a leather jacket and carry a gun. You chase after bad guys and could have your choice of badge bunny. If I looked up the term 'bad boy' in the dictionary, I suspect your picture might be there. Rumors around the station run rampant about you and your exploits."

"Good. My master plan is working. I have you completely fooled." His eyes smoldered devilishly, and my stomach flipped, wondering what he was thinking. "By the way, Officer Sarconi, there are some rumors running rampant at the station about you too."

"Really?" I had heard most of them, but I was intrigued to hear what he was about to say.

"Apparently, you have an insatiable appetite for ruggedly handsome detectives." He scooted closer and pressed himself against me.

"Shut up." The laugh escaped my lips, even if he was being cheesy. "So what's the final tally? Who mentioned work the most today?"

"Me."

I narrowed my eyes at him. "You cheated. You wanted to lose."

He grinned and ducked beneath the covers. I inhaled sharply, feeling his warm breath against my leg, and then the phone rang.

"Did you dial my cell phone just to screw this up?" he asked, but before I could answer, my phone went off too. "I can't catch a break tonight."

"Really? *You* can't catch a break?"

He snickered at the angry look on my face and

grabbed his phone off the dresser while I did the same. It was the station. I moved into the living room to talk in private.

Word had traveled that I had revisited the crime scene this afternoon. Due to a recent development, I was being summoned to answer questions. When I disconnected, Michael was hovering in the doorway.

"They're calling you in too?" he asked.

"Yes, but no one said exactly why. Were we discovered? Is this about our relationship?"

"They wouldn't call us in after midnight for something that insignificant. Who are you supposed to report to?"

"Lieutenant Peterson."

"I'm meeting Jack and Samantha. Do you have anything else you can change into besides the dress from earlier and my clothes?"

"I have a t-shirt and jeans in my bag."

"Okay, lock-up when you leave. I'll meet you back here whenever this gets sorted out."

"Riley," I said, stopping him in his tracks. He hated it when I used his last name when we were off the clock or speaking privately. "What happened that's so urgent?"

"If you're supposed to know, the lieutenant will tell you. If not, I'll tell you when we get home." It wasn't the answer I wanted, but Michael was dressed and out the door before I could ask another question.

When I arrived at the station, Lieutenant Peterson had an officer waiting to escort me into his office. The only time this many officers worked graveyard was when something horrible happened.

"Sir?" I took the offered chair in front of his desk.

"Officer Sarconi, why did you visit Mr. Cline today?"

"I wanted to follow up with the investigation from

the other night. It just so happened I ran into Detective Riley who had been tasked with picking up a form for Detective Lightman, so Riley let me tag along."

"What time did you leave the jewelry store?"

"Around five."

"Did Detective Riley leave when you did?"

"Yes." Shit, this sounded like it was about our relationship.

"Did you notice anyone else in the vicinity during your time with Cline or when you were leaving?"

"No, sir. I walked the perimeter, per the detective's request. No one was around."

"Thanks, Sarconi. You're dismissed." He jerked his chin at the door, and I got up to leave. Before I cleared the doorframe, he spoke again. "According to the roll call records, you called in sick today. Why were you following up?"

"I was feeling better and wanted to earn back some brownie points after that civilian complaint." It wasn't exactly true, but it sounded reasonable. Too bad it also made me sound like a brown-noser.

"Don't let crap like that get to you, and don't do something like this again."

"Yes, sir." I practically broke into a run to get out of there before he could ask anything else.

On my way out, Kemper spotted me. He excused himself from the conversation he was having with Officer Hawking and made a beeline toward me. I pretended not to notice, but he blocked my path to the exit.

"Hey, Lexie. I thought you weren't coming in tonight." He glanced around and lowered his voice. "I was going to call in sick with the blue flu to teach the brass a lesson for suspending us, but I figured that's exactly what they wanted me to do. Are you working undercover or something?" He studied my casual clothes.

"I had to come in to answer questions. Now, I'm going home. Why are there so many officers on duty? It looks like half of day shift stuck around."

"You didn't hear what happened?"

"What?"

"One of the shop owners who was helping identify the crew behind the recent string of robberies was found dead outside his store."

I broke out in a cold sweat. "Who?"

"I don't know. They haven't told us much, other than to watch our backs. Officer Cruise was hurt last night on duty, and now a witness has been murdered. We're working under the assumption it's the same crew who committed the break-ins, but the brass has us doubling up on patrols and radioing for backup whenever we respond to a call, just to be on the safe side. The watch commander's afraid the Skulls have declared war on the police. So we're being careful."

"Is this about the bullet in the alleyway?"

Kemper pressed his lips together. "Maybe that bang was more than we realized."

"We were lucky."

"That's how the brass is acting. Homicide's been sniffing around, but I don't think they want to take the case away from gangs." He studied my appearance. "I didn't mean to talk your head off. You should go home. You're not looking so good. Are you really sick?"

"I think I might be."

TWELVE

I returned to Michael's apartment, but I didn't expect to see him again tonight. Mr. Cline was dead, and there was a very good chance we had been the last two people to see him alive. I didn't know Cline from a hole in the wall. Shouldn't his last few hours have been spent with family and friends instead of two cops who would have preferred being anywhere else?

To distract myself, I went into the bedroom in search of my discarded belongings. Five minutes later, I had my clothes and toiletries packed. My gun and badge were in my purse, but I looked again to make sure I hadn't forgotten anything. Then I went to the table to scribble a note, saying I had gone home. Before I could sign my name, Michael came home.

"Lexie," he called, "I'm back."

"I was just about to leave," I said in response to the curious look he was giving my bags. "Was it Cline? No one said, but it must have been him. That's the only thing that makes any sense. Was he killed?"

"Yes." Michael pressed his lips together. "Why are you leaving?"

"I figured you'd be working through the night with Lightman and Preston."

"Jack and Sam went home too. We need a fresh set

of eyes to look at these facts. Normal break-ins don't turn violent. The offenders have been hitting these establishments in the middle of the night when no one is around. They aren't interested in civilian casualties, but they may be interested in taking out the cops who respond to the alarms, like Officer Cruise."

"What exactly happened last night?"

"Cruise had just concluded a call nearby. He showed up sooner than they expected and surprised the thieves. He nearly had one of the men in cuffs when the other one came at him with a bat. They broke his leg and his ribs." Michael's fists clenched, his jaw muscles flexing. "The brass doesn't believe that attack was premeditated. The weapon was something they had with them to break into the display cases, but what they did to Mr. Cline was cold-blooded murder. They waited to get him alone, and then they killed him."

"Why? You just said they didn't want to harm civilians."

"Things change. Cline wanted to help us stop them."

"Kemper said homicide was checking into it."

"They are." Michael's blue eyes resembled flames. He double-checked the locks on his front door and took a seat at the kitchen table. "Did you notice anyone when we were at the jewelry store? You checked outside. Maybe you spotted someone paying too much attention or staking out the place."

"I didn't."

"Are you positive?"

"I do this for a living," I snapped, regretting my tone instantly. I slumped into the chair next to Michael. "Cline's dead, and we were there."

"I know." The unstated fact floated in the space between us. If we hadn't left when we did, maybe

Cline wouldn't have been killed. Michael went to the liquor cabinet and took out a bottle of tequila and two glasses. "I shouldn't have brought you there. What did Peterson want?"

"He wanted to know why I was there, when we left, and if I saw anything." I drank the shot Michael placed in front of me in a single gulp. "What time was Cline killed?"

"The coroner doesn't have an exact TOD yet, but based on Cline's security logs, the system reengaged after seven. He was supposed to meet his wife at the movies at nine, but he never made it. So somewhere in that two hour window. I'm guessing it was closer to seven. The security footage should prove it. We just need to find a camera that had a good angle. Maybe we'll get lucky and ID the perps that way."

"Where did they find his body?" I refilled the shot glasses, swallowing again. "Was he right outside his shop?"

"This isn't your investigation, Lexie. We shouldn't be talking about this. You aren't involved. Not yet, not unless Jack signs off, and I don't think you should ask to assist on the case. Not now. Not after this."

"Why the hell not? I'm a cop. One of our own was attacked, and the guy we interviewed this afternoon was killed. This is on us."

"No, it's not. It's on me." Michael slammed his glass down. He focused the anger and intensity on me. "I'm serious. I don't want you involved. I mean it."

"You don't get to tell me that."

"They tried to kill you once. I don't want them to get a second chance."

"The bullet in the alley?"

"What else would I be talking about?"

I glared at him. "Kemper said they found Cline outside his store. Is it true?"

"Why don't you ask Kemper?"

"I'm asking you. I am not your enemy, but I need to know where Cline was found."

"Five feet from the back door. They bashed his brains in with a tire iron. Are you happy now?"

"What the fuck's wrong with you?" My eye twitched, and a tear ran down my cheek.

Michael rubbed a hand down his face. "Honey, I'm sorry. It was a shit day."

"No, it wasn't, but it went to shit." And it made me feel guilty for every fun moment we had after leaving Cline's shop. I stood, feeling the effects of the tequila. Teetering into the bedroom, I collapsed on the bed seconds before I started to cry. I barely even knew the man, but it bothered me. It bothered Michael too. That's why we were fighting.

Michael entered the room and pulled me against his chest. "I know, Lexie. We were there. We should have done something." He hesitated. "We'll get them. I promise. It won't matter how many threatening notes they leave because they won't get away with this. If you want in, we'll take them down together." He held me tightly until I cried myself to sleep.

~*~

The next day was business as usual. Michael got up that morning for work, and I left at the same time he did so I could spend the rest of the day in my apartment before reporting for duty. Michael and I hadn't spoken much. Everything was still too fresh and raw. We didn't need to fight with each other or rehash yesterday's tragedy.

When I got home, I ran eight miles on the treadmill, showered, and cleaned my apartment. It didn't make the guilt or anger go away. So I vacuumed with a vengeance and spent the rest of the day trying to study, but my mind kept drifting. Hopefully, I knew all the codes and techniques by now. But the voice in the back of my head said if I was a half-decent cop, Mr. Cline wouldn't be dead. Maybe that's why Michael didn't want me assisting on this case. Maybe I distracted him. But deep down, I knew this wasn't my fault. The voice in my head was nothing more than my own self-doubt and guilt.

"Shut up," I growled. Now I was talking to myself. Maybe I was crazy. The department would surely frown on that.

When I couldn't take the silence of my apartment for another moment, I went to the station. I hoped to talk things out with Michael and see what Lightman had to say, but I didn't spot any familiar faces. Preston, Devereaux, Riley, and Lightman were all out of the office. Now what happened?

At roll call, Lieutenants Peterson and Chloe Ames, the female homicide lieutenant I'd worked with while undercover for vice, took over the briefing the watch commander was giving. Every officer in the room sat up straighter. The chitchat and snickers came to an immediate halt. This was serious.

Lt. Peterson hit the lights and turned on the projector. "As some of you may have heard, two nights ago, Officer Cruise was attacked while responding to a crime in progress. His assailants wore dark clothes and had gas masks, shielding their faces from his view. When Cruise entered, he only spotted a single suspect. A second suspect came out of the shadows." Peterson paused the surveillance footage on the screen before we had to watch the assault play out in real time. "The doctors say Officer Cruise is expected to make a full recovery once his leg and ribs have time to mend. However, the suspects escaped. We believe they've already escalated."

"What does that mean?" someone asked.

"A jewelry store owner was killed last night." Peterson glanced at me before his eyes roamed over the rest of the room. "Mr. Cline, the store owner, had agreed to provide his security records, work orders, and surveillance footage to our detectives. Believing someone from the security company was involved, Mr. Cline offered to identify the men who had installed the security system and performed work in his shop. A couple of hours after we visited him to collect these records, someone took a tire iron to Cline's skull." Peterson placed the crime scene photos on the projector.

Bile rose in my throat, and I looked away.

"How do we know it was the thieves and not some other psychopath?" Hawking asked.

"Homicide is exploring that possibility, but we're fairly certain it's the same crew since they left a second calling card." Peterson changed the photos on the projector. Beneath another graffiti tag of a crowned skull were scrawled the words *casualty of war*. "You were briefed yesterday about the threat the Skulls have leveled against the police department. Until the killer or killers are apprehended, no one leaves here without a partner. If you respond to a call that fits these fuckers' MO, radio for backup before engaging. Do not endanger yourselves. We will nail these assholes, but we're going to be safe and smart about it." He took a deep breath. "Are there any questions?" Silence filled the room. "Okay, get to work."

"Dammit," I swore.

"What's wrong?" Hawking asked. "Are you okay?"

"I went to see Cline yesterday. I thought I should make sure we didn't miss anything. Detective Riley was there too, but we didn't stop Cline from being killed. In fact, maybe our presence is the reason he was killed."

"You can't blame yourself. You had no way of knowing about any of this. I bet those assholes didn't even show up until you were long gone." Hawking looked grim. "We're supposed to prevent crimes from happening, but that's a joke. You know that as well as I do. We get called in after shit happens, and we clean up the mess. How would we know where dirtbags are or what they intend to do? This isn't *Minority Report*. We're not psychic, and we can't make an arrest until the law is broken. The system sucks, but it's the only one we have. So we soldier on."

"Soldier on? Really, Hawking? You're former military. Isn't that a little on the nose for you to say?"

"It cheered you up, didn't it?" He grinned. "Shouldn't you get going? I'm working the desk, so you're riding with Kemper tonight."

"Crap." I grabbed my gear and raced down the hallway.

"Sarconi," Kemper waved me over to our assigned patrol car, "I thought you abandoned me."

"I'd never do anything like that. Even though, this case sucks."

"Being on the front lines sucks even more." He opened the car door. "After our civilian complaint, we're on the lieutenant's shit list. Under different circumstances, we'd be on desk duty and not working together. Instead, we're getting sent into the line of fire and expected to be courteous and professional while some shitheads try to slaughter us."

"Don't say things like that."

"You're the one who pointed out the crooks lured us to that alleyway and tried to shoot us." Kemper sighed. "Me. The asshole tried to shoot me."

"You don't know that."

"Don't I? You knew from the start. You knew that second night we canvassed."

"Bobby, come on."

He grinned, but it didn't reach his eyes. "So that's how I get you to say my name. What is that, Lex? Pity?"

"No."

Kemper jerked his chin in the direction of the gangs unit. "I guess it's a good thing we didn't volunteer to help Lightman out since these assholes already have our number."

"Don't tell me you changed your mind. I may have mentioned something to Riley yesterday about putting a good word in for us with Lightman." But I didn't know if Michael followed through, and I wasn't sure if he should.

THIRTEEN

The radio call interrupted our conversation. A twenty-four hour convenience store had just been robbed. Glancing at Kemper, I hit the lights and headed for the location while he radioed back that we were responding.

We were the first car that arrived. The call didn't fit the profile of the other crimes, so there was no reason for us to request backup. I left the lights on, parking diagonally in front of the shop, partially on the sidewalk. There wasn't a soul in sight.

Cautiously, Kemper entered the store, and I brought up the rear. The owner was clearly shaken, pacing behind the register with a baseball bat in his hand. He gave us an exasperated look and launched into a rapid-fire rendition of what happened.

Three men had entered the store. Two of them went to the beer fridge and smashed the bottles, distracting the owner. While he was busy confronting the two, the third man went behind the counter and cleaned out the register.

"Are there any additional details you can recall?" I asked. He shook his head, annoyed with himself. "What about the surveillance camera?" I pointed to the camera posted above the register.

"It doesn't work. The power cord is faulty. I haven't gotten around to buying a new one." The owner looked even gloomier. "Guess there's no need anymore."

Kemper investigated the broken beer bottles and the rest of the store for evidence.

"Sir, you can talk to a sketch artist in the morning. Maybe he can make a composite, so we can find the men responsible," I said.

"Hooligans. Little, snot-nosed, wannabe gangbangers is what they were." He was getting worked up again. "They wanted to be thugs, wearing chains and those baggy pants that show their butt cracks. Dumbass kids."

"We'll file a report. You can pick up a copy while you're there." The biggest downfall of the job was not being able to do much after a crime was committed, especially when we had an unreliable eyewitness and no camera footage. "Kemper, did you find anything?" I called, excusing myself.

"Nothing." He lingered near the back refrigerators, crouching down. "I don't get why they smashed the beer. It was the imported stuff too."

"They didn't care about the beer. They wanted the money."

"But they touched glass bottles. Don't you think we might be able to pull their prints from the shards?"

"Possibly. From what the owner said, they wanted to prove they were tough. I doubt they wore gloves."

Kemper counted the broken necks and caps. "They took some with them. There are two empty cardboard containers and only nine tops." He snorted. "One each."

"I guess they wanted to toast their success. C'mon, let's finish taking the clerk's statement and get their descriptions out. It's the best we can do."

After we left the store, we drove around the area, hoping to spot someone who fit the storekeeper's description. Just as we were about to head back to the station and conclude our shift, dispatch came over the radio with another reported break-in two blocks from our location. Two men had been seen ransacking a liquor store.

Kemper picked up the radio. "We'll check it out."

An uneasy feeling settled in the pit of my stomach. Something was off about this one. "Radio back and find out who called in the crime in progress. The liquor store closed eight hours ago, and it isn't in a residential area. Who was around to make the call?"

"Someone passing by probably heard the ruckus." Kemper caught the concerned look on my face. "I'll ask anyway. I don't want you to be scared."

"Jackass."

He chuckled, waiting for dispatch to respond to the question. "Do you think the owner will reward our diligence with a bottle of Patron or Grey Goose? My liquor cabinet could use some restocking."

"You know that's against regulations."

"Yeah, I know," Kemper said. "I was joking."

The radio squawked to life, informing us the tip came from an anonymous caller. That did nothing to quell my fears. I asked for an ETA on our backup. Ten minutes.

Coming to a stop in front of the store, Kemper and I got out of the car. My hand rested on the butt of my gun as we crept toward the front door. Backup was on the way, but a lot could happen in ten minutes. Until then, this was our show.

Shadows moved within the store. I couldn't tell what they were holding, but they had something. Drawing my weapon and turning on my flashlight, I stepped through the broken glass of the front door.

"Police. Freeze," I announced. Nothing about this scene was like the break-in at the jewelry store, but that didn't mean it wasn't dangerous.

The interior was dark. The only illumination came from a single neon sign hanging above a cooler. A figure moved to the right. I shifted, focusing on him.

Kemper moved behind me, spotting a second man. "Hands in the air," he said.

In the darkness, I couldn't see much of their faces. I aimed the beam of my flashlight higher. The thug looked familiar with ink creeping up over his collar. He smirked, causing flashes from two nights ago to play through my mind. It appeared to be the same tattoo, but this was a different man.

"Don't make any sudden moves," Kemper ordered.

The men raised their hands, dropping the extra large vodka bottles they were holding. The glass shattered on the floor, making a large puddle.

"Oops," the one in front of me said. "Do you want me to clean that up?" He started to lower his arms.

"Keep your hands up and slowly put them on top of your head," I said.

"Interlock your fingers behind your head," Kemper added. He moved closer to the second suspect, spun him around, and pushed him against the wall. "Lex, I'll cover you. Go ahead and cuff him."

The last thing I wanted to do was get that close to these guys, but I didn't have a choice. The sooner we got them cuffed, the sooner we could stick them in the back of our car before checking the rest of the place.

While Kemper covered me, I stepped forward to slap the cuffs on the suspect. Before I could reach him, a third guy emerged from the shadows, shoved Kemper, and bolted for the door.

"I got him," my partner yelled, forgetting he was covering me.

Instantly, the room darkened as Kemper turned toward the third suspect, his flashlight no longer aimed in my direction. An entire shelf careened to the floor. More glass bottles hit the ground. The only sound besides glass shattering was the squeak of Kemper's shoes.

The suspect stopped at the broken door, grabbed the metal door handle, and swung himself to the side. The metal doorframe slammed into the center of Kemper's face and body, knocking him backward with a resounding oomph.

But the suspect didn't run. He launched himself at Kemper. The first kick made me cringe. I had to help my partner. I aimed at the man attacking him.

"Stop, or I'll shoot." I never expected such cliched words to come out of my mouth, but there they were.

The suspect stopped mid-kick, raised his hands to waist height, and chuckled. Blood ran down the center of Kemper's face, but the hit from the door wasn't enough to keep him down. Once his feet were underneath him, he pounced, tackling the suspect and forcing him onto his stomach.

I turned back to the other two men, aware that they had moved closer. This wasn't good. We were outnumbered and possibly outgunned.

"Don't move," I warned, stepping backward, closer to Kemper. My partner needed help. I shifted my aim from one man to the other, but in the dark, they were nothing more than shadows.

Kemper grunted, struggling to keep the third suspect down.

"Do you have him?" I asked.

"Not yet."

I cautioned a glance over my shoulder. Kemper was fighting to keep the guy on his stomach. The crunch of glass told me the other two suspects had moved again.

Closer or farther away? I whipped my flashlight beam toward them. "Get on your knees. Hands on your head. I won't ask again."

As quickly as I could, I slapped cuffs onto one of them and hooked him to the shelving. When I turned toward the other one, I found him slinking toward the rear of the liquor store.

"I said don't move." Where was our backup?

"Gun," Kemper yelled a moment before a gunshot rang out behind me.

FOURTEEN

Kemper tried to wrestle the gun away from the suspect, the weapon aimed in the air as the two men struggled for control of it. With the way they were locked together, I couldn't risk firing a shot. I could accidentally hit Kemper.

Instead, instincts kicked in, and I barreled into the third suspect, knocking him off my partner. The gun clattered across the floor and disappeared into the dark abyss. I didn't know if that had been Kemper's gun or the suspect's.

The third suspect wouldn't go down easy. He grabbed my upper arms, squeezing hard enough to leave bruises, before using our combined momentum to slam me into the side of the counter. The register crashed down beside us, forcing me to roll out of the way.

I was halfway to my feet when someone kicked me hard enough in the side to send me sliding across the slick, wet floor. The surprise and adrenaline kept me from feeling the initial impact, but once I stopped moving, a sharp pain shot through me. Dragging myself up, I reached for my flashlight and gun.

Kemper grabbed the third suspect, shoved him into the wall, and handcuffed him. Two down. One to go.

"You okay?" Kemper asked, his flashlight beam darting from left to right.

"Where is he?" I whispered, unsure where the other suspect had gone.

"He's here somewhere." Kemper wiped blood from his face with the back of his hand.

Another bottle crashed to the ground in the vicinity of the man I'd handcuffed. Kemper and I shone our flashlights in that direction.

Letting the barrel of my gun lead the way, I moved deeper into the store. Dangling from the shelf were my handcuffs. Before I could say a word, another gunshot rang out.

I turned and watched Kemper crumple to the ground. The man who shot Kemper fired again, hitting Kemper in the chest before running for the front door. I fired several shots, losing count and unsure if any of them hit their mark.

Kemper grabbed onto the suspect's fleeing ankle, an anguished cry coming from deep within. The suspect dragged Kemper halfway out the front door before kicking his leg free. He yanked the door hard, slamming it into Kemper's body. I raced toward the exit, firing again.

"Kemper, talk to me," I said, my eyes on the darkness in front of me.

Glass crunched to the right, but there wasn't time to react before someone grabbed me. I bucked and fought. But he was too strong. He knocked the gun from my hand before yanking me back into the depths of the liquor store. He threw me to the ground, and I slid, banging into the shelves.

My gun and flashlight were gone. The only thing I had left was my radio.

"Kemper?" I screamed. Reaching for my radio with my non-dominant hand, I pressed the button. "Shots fired. Officer down. Request immediate assistance. Send backup. All available units."

"You shouldn't have done that," a disembodied voice said from the other side of the store.

I shifted into a defensive stance. I had to keep my wits about me, but more importantly, I needed to get to Kemper. He'd been shot. He was hurt, possibly dying.

The offender, the one with the tattoo, moved toward me. He was at least half a foot taller and fifty pounds heavier than me. "Looks like you're all alone now."

"Get on the ground," I said.

"Why don't you make me?"

"On the ground," I repeated, my focus split between him and the shadows surrounding us. The other man was still inside. Kemper had handcuffed him near the door, but I wasn't sure he was still there.

"You can't shoot me." He laughed again. "You lost your gun."

"I said get on the ground."

"What's a matter, baby? Scared of the dark?" the other voice taunted.

I kept alternating my gaze, but there were too many places to look. But the voice didn't come from near the door, where Kemper had handcuffed him. It came from somewhere to my left, somewhere much closer.

A shelf crashed to the ground, forcing me to shield myself from the cascade of liquor bottles, which exploded on the floor around me in a blast of glass and spirits. While I was distracted, the one with the tattoo grabbed me from behind. He held me in a tight bear hug. His strong, thick arms encompassed my body, forcing my hands down at my sides.

I struggled and kicked, desperate to get free. Without the use of my arms and lack of leverage due to the height difference, there wasn't much I could do to hurt the guy. I tried to swing my body around, but his grip was too tight.

I bucked more fiercely, throwing off his center of gravity. He stumbled backward. His back hit something solid. The wall, probably. I fought as hard as I could. The back of my head slammed into his chest, but it had no effect on the hold he had on me.

The other one emerged from the shadows, laughing as I desperately fought to get free.

"Kemper," I yelled, hoping he was alive and could assist.

"Looks like game over for your partner," the man in front of me said. "Such a shame." He reached out to touch my face, and I tried to bite him.

He backhanded me across the cheek hard enough that I tasted blood. "Bitch, I'll knock your fucking teeth out."

The threat distracted the guy holding me, and I stomped down on his foot. He howled, his grip loosening. But he didn't let me go. I managed to turn my body sideways, giving me a little more space to work with. Then I jabbed my elbow into his solar plexus, knocking the wind out of him with an oof.

I broke free, but the other man was already on top of me. He knocked into me like a brick wall, forcing me flush against him. I could barely breathe, but he kept squeezing. I pushed against his chin, trying to get away. But it didn't work, so I went for his throat.

I couldn't get a grip. My nails cut into his skin, causing him to hiss. He wrapped his arms around me like a boa constrictor, squeezing until my vision swam and my ribs popped, on the verge of snapping.

"Help," I screamed.

"Shut her up," the human boa constrictor said.

Something hard collided with the back of my head,

and the world flipped upside down. The pressure eased from my ribcage as I dropped onto the wet floor. The glass shards cut into my palms, but I barely noticed. The pain came in waves. Something warm and sticky spread over me. Keeping my eyes open got harder by the second.

I saw Kemper lying on the ground, half in the store, half on the sidewalk. He had yet to move. I had to get to him. We had to get out of here.

"What should we do with her?" one of them asked.

"I know what I'd like to do to her," the one with the tattoo said.

Lifting onto my hands and knees, I crawled a few inches before I fell back to the ground, too dizzy to try that again. Dragging my body forward, using my forearms, I slid toward the exit. My hand brushed against Kemper's pant leg, but before I could pull myself closer or get out the door, one of the men grabbed me and dragged me away from the front door. The liquor soaked into my clothes, and the glass shredded my uniform and cut my exposed skin.

"Where do you think you're going?" The tattooed guy grabbed my ankle and pulled me into the dark recesses of the liquor store.

The smell of spirits nauseated me and made my eyes burn. I shut them against the pain. It didn't matter since I couldn't see anything anyway, but I feared I may never open them again.

When I felt someone's breath against my cheek, I attacked blindly. My desperate swings made contact. I heard a crunch, followed by cursing.

"Hold her down." The voice was angrier now. "She broke my nose. She's gonna pay for that."

I fought as hard as I could, opening my eyes but seeing nothing but darkness. Someone grabbed my hands and pressed them into the ground beside me.

How could they see when I couldn't? I didn't understand.

The pain and dizziness hit harder, triggering a sense of falling even though I was already on the ground. My stomach lurched, but I swallowed the bile, twisting my hips even as a knee pressed into my thigh and a heel banged against the shin of my other leg, forcing me to remain still.

Hands went to my belt, roughly unhooking and tugging on it. I grunted, the fight draining from me. "We don't have time for that," the other one hissed. "She called for backup. They'll be here soon."

"Don't you think I know that?" He bound my hands together with my belt, pulling it tight until the leather cut into my wrists.

I blinked out, my grasp on consciousness decreasing by the second. My head hurt too much for me to feel anything else, or so I thought until something so cold it felt white-hot tore into my arm. I screamed. More laughter ensued, and then they were gone.

The pain in my arm helped me focus. When the echoing thuds of their footsteps faded into oblivion, I rolled onto my side. My arms were useless where they remained bound. But I had to get outside. I had to get to Kemper. I didn't know if he was alive or dead, but I had to help him.

I wriggled like a worm, inching toward the door, the pain in my arm getting worse as I used the outside of my forearm to drag my body across the treacherous wet floor. After what felt like an eternity, I spotted Kemper.

With one final heave, I made it to the broken doorframe. "Kemper, answer me."

"Lexie?" I heard the pain and confusion in his voice. Or maybe I imagined it.

Hold on, I thought, but I didn't have the strength to say it. The sound of sirens made me relax, and I let my eyes close.

FIFTEEN

"I need help over here."

I knew that voice. "Michael?" I opened my eyes, but I couldn't see anything but a beam of light against the dark backdrop.

"Try not to move, babe. I'm here. Everything's going to be okay. I got you." He knelt beside me, brushing my wet hair back and shining the light in my eyes. He took off his jacket and balled it up before gently slipping it beneath my head and releasing my bound arms.

"Kemper," I gasped, struggling to get up.

"Shh." Michael knelt over me, assessing my injuries. "Stay there."

"He was shot. He—" My breathing became more frantic, and I tried to roll over, but a stabbing pain in my side stopped me.

Michael stared out the front door. "He's alive, Lex. The EMTs are working on him now." He inhaled. "Hurry it up. She's in bad shape. She needs help too."

I closed my eyes. That was all that mattered.

"Hey, don't do that. I need you to stay awake. Look at me, Lexie." Michael touched my cheek, but that wasn't enough to convince me to open my eyes. Suddenly, a sharp pain exploded through my arm, and my eyes shot open. Michael pressed down against the inside of my forearm.

I curled in on myself, crying out in pain.

"I'm sorry, Lex. I'm so sorry." He yelled again for help, and I closed my eyes against the agony.

"Careful," a voice said as I felt myself being rolled. The motion made my stomach churn, and I vomited. A bright light shone into my eyes. "She has a concussion."

"Why do you think they carved that?" another voice asked. Was that Detective Preston speaking?

"Hang on, we need to photograph what we can. I'll send a crime tech with you. They might have left evidence on her," Lightman said.

"How the hell did this happen?" That voice belonged to Michael. "Two cars per call. That's what we said."

The voices and questions made no sense. They swirled around, getting lost in the agonizing abyss. A hand pressed against my stomach, and my eyes shot open.

"Easy. You're okay," a paramedic said. "We're gonna get you fixed up." He looked at someone behind me. "Radio ahead that she might have internal bleeding. The trauma unit should be aware and standing by."

"Kemper?" I asked again.

"Your partner?" the paramedic asked.

"They shot him."

"He's okay. Another team is taking care of him."

Kemper was okay. That meant I could close my eyes again.

"Hey, stay with me, Officer Sarconi," the paramedic said.

My eyes fluttered, and I fought to keep them open. But it was a losing battle. At least my arm didn't hurt as much anymore.

"Alessandra, stay awake," the paramedic said. The gurney bumped against something, sending excruciating jolts through my body. The sun had come up, and it was too bright. Everything was too bright and too loud. Sleep. That's all I needed. "Alessandra? Alessandra?"

"Her name's Lexie," Michael said.

"Go with her," Preston said. "Update us as soon as you can."

"Will do," Michael replied.

~*~

When I opened my eyes again, vertigo had set in. The floor moved toward the ceiling, making me cling to the side of the bed for fear of falling off the edge when the world tipped sideways. I couldn't figure out why things were moving like this.

The room was drab white with pale green. It felt like I was on a boat, but I had no idea how that could have happened. It hurt to breathe, and even the slightest movement seemed like a very bad idea. I swung my arm out, making contact with someone as I rolled onto my back, hoping the bed wouldn't pitch and throw me to the ground.

"Thank god, you're awake," Michael said, emotion filling his voice. "I'm right here." He gently took my hand in his.

I turned to look at him, which made the room spin. Squeezing my eyes closed, I grasped his hand harder. "What happened? Where are we?"

"You're in the hospital."

"What?" Memories flooded back to me, the panic setting in. "Kemper?"

"He's fine for now. He had his vest on. He'll

survive."

"I saw him go down. The asshole shot him and ran off. I tried to stop him. I tried, but—"

"Hey," Michael grasped my face. "This isn't your fault. They ambushed you. You did the best you could. You called for help and fought to survive. You did good. Jack was impressed. We all are."

"Did you catch the guy?"

"Guys. Kemper said there were three of them." Michael looked concerned. "Do you remember what happened? Anything you can tell us will help."

I squinted against the harsh light, my vision blurry. Michael released my hand and crossed the room, flipping off the light. At the sudden darkness, my eyes shot open, and despite the torment that quick action inflicted within my skull, I remembered the men inside the liquor store.

"There were two of them. They came at me. They wouldn't let me go. I should have shot them, but I lost my gun. Kemper was already down. We couldn't stop them." I gasped in between the words. "We only saw two. We missed the third. It was too dark. When he jumped Kemper, everything went to hell."

"Shh, Lexie," Michael soothed, "it's okay. You did all you could. The best you could. You fought hard. The techs found blood at the scene that wasn't yours. You got a piece of one of them at least."

"I broke his nose. I may have shot another one."

"Good. We can use that to identify them and track them down."

"They set us up. It was a trap." A thought nearly formed, but I couldn't quite access it. "Dammit. Why can't I think straight?"

"Slow, deep breaths. C'mon, babe, you have to relax." Michael's eyes flicked to the machine behind me. "Focus on me, Lex. Everything's going to be okay.

I promise."

I winced with each breath, but his blue eyes ripped through the fog. "Do you think this was another ambush? They didn't have masks or spray paint like the Skulls."

"I don't know." Michael brushed my hair out of my face. "We'll figure it out. When Jack heard the call over the radio for all available units, we came running. We should have gotten there sooner. I should have gotten to you sooner."

"Lightman?"

Michael snickered, more from nerves than at my ignorance. "Yes, Lexie. Detective Jack Lightman."

"That was his voice. I couldn't see him, but I knew the voice was familiar." I closed my eyes, recalling bits and pieces. When I opened them again, everything was still fuzzy. "What's wrong with me? What did they do to me?"

"The doctors ran a lot of tests. We're waiting on a few of the results. Amber's been making sure they don't screw anything up. She assigned the best doctors and nurses to take care of you." He offered a smile that didn't make it to his eyes. "You have a concussion."

"That explains the dizzy and the blurry."

Michael leaned in closer. "Can you see me?"

I reached for his face, surprised by the bandages covering my arm.

He kissed my cheek and gently nuzzled against me. "Tell me what hurts."

"Everything. Nothing. I don't know. My arm really stings."

"Okay."

The door opened, and the overhead light turned on. I winced but forced my eyes to remain open. Michael turned at the intrusion.

"The doc needs to check on the patient." Detective Samantha Preston offered a tight smile. "Glad to see you're awake and alive, Sarconi."

"Thanks."

She nodded before giving Michael a pointed look. "Can I have a word with you?"

"In a minute," Michael said. "I want to be here for this."

The doctor stepped around Preston, flipping through my chart. "I'm Dr. Flanagan." He hovered over the bed, causing me to turn my head to the other side and endure another round of room spins. "It seems you've had quite the unpleasant morning, Officer Sarconi. How are you feeling?"

"Not great."

"I can imagine." He ran through a list of rudimentary questions, marked something on the chart, and took out a penlight. "You're not going to like this, but I'll make it quick." He flashed the light in my eyes and asked me to follow his finger.

"If you expect me to read an eye chart, it starts with an E. But don't expect me to see anything beyond that."

"Hopefully, that'll clear up in a couple of days. The dizziness should subside sooner. We'll keep an eye on things. But you're lucky. A hit like that to the back of the head can cause serious issues." He put some films on the lightboard and turned it on. "We've taken several sets of scans. We'll keep you a few days to monitor the situation, but things are looking good. If your scans remain clear, you should be able to go home soon. Right now, a brain bleed is our biggest concern."

"How likely is that, Doc?" Michael asked.

"Her last CT scan was clear, which was an obvious improvement over the first. The x-ray was also clean.

No skull fractures. So that's good. If you wouldn't mind stepping into the hallway, so I can finish up."

Michael gently ran his hand down the edge of the bandage on my arm. "I'll be right outside."

The doctor rolled the blanket down a few inches and gingerly touched my ribs and stomach.

"Shit."

"The x-rays didn't show any breaks, but you have some serious bruises. Do you remember how this happened?"

"Someone kicked me."

The doctor put a new set of films onto the lightboard. "Everything looks about as good as can be expected. You'll be swollen and bruised for a while, but the internal bleeding has stopped. You should be okay. The best thing you can do is get some rest."

SIXTEEN

"Hey, Sarconi," Detective Samantha Preston stepped into my hospital room, giving Michael a warning look before turning her attention back to me, "I heard you're getting discharged."

It had been three days. I was more than ready to go home. "Yeah."

She pulled out her notepad. "I was hoping you might have remembered something else about the men who attacked you."

"I already told you everything. It was dark and hard to see. The tattoo was the only thing familiar about them." I sat up a little higher in the bed, glad to be wearing regular clothes, courtesy of Amber, rather than the hospital gown that wouldn't stay closed.

"How many of them were tattooed?"

"Just the one, I think."

She nodded.

"We've gone over this a million times, Sam." Michael shifted in his seat where he'd been ever since I was attacked. "She told you everything. What did you get off the surveillance footage?"

"They disconnected the interior cameras when they arrived. We got a few shots of them, but they kept their faces down. We didn't get a good enough angle to make an ID."

"What about security footage from the sex shop?" I asked. "That happened a week ago, but—"

"We've pulled it," Preston said. "But you already said you didn't recognize the assailants as the same men you spoke to that night."

"No, but it'll give you a better idea of his tattoo."

She licked her lips. "Why don't you describe it for me in detail?"

I did the best I could, but with half the ink concealed beneath the men's collars, I couldn't give her all the details.

"Lexie isn't making it up," Michael said.

"I didn't say she was."

Michael's eyes narrowed. "Not in those exact words—"

"Not in any words." Preston sighed and put her notepad away. "Jack wants you to sit with a sketch artist. But we'll give you a few more days to recover."

"I don't need more time. I can do this now. Today. Whatever."

"Tomorrow," she said, "if you're feeling up to it."

"I hate this."

"I know." She pressed her lips together. "The concussion will keep you out for at least a week. You've served half of that time here. Depending on how you feel and what medical has to say, Jack's hoping you'll be back on desk duty soon. If you want, that is."

"Why?"

She smiled. "He figured you'd want in on catching these assholes."

"Absolutely."

"Sam," Michael warned.

"It's not up to you. We already talked about this." She stepped toward the door. "Get well soon. We'll keep a seat warm for you."

"Thanks, Detective Preston."

She nodded and let herself out of the room.

Michael stood, intent on going after her, but I grabbed his arm. "Don't," I said. "I want this, and she knows it. How would you handle this situation if you were in my place?"

Something dark crossed behind Michael's eyes. "I'd put the fuckers in the ground."

~*~

My balance was off, and it had a direct line to my unsettled stomach. Michael gently lifted me into his arms and carried me up the stairs to my apartment before setting me down on the bed.

"You need to rest, but you also need to eat something," he said.

I was too nauseous to think about food. I smelled like a cross between hospital disinfectant and a distillery. The smell of tequila still clung to my hair and skin, making the queasiness worse. I'd never gotten car sick before, but the bright lights and stop-go motion hadn't been pleasant. "I'm not hungry."

"You haven't eaten in days. You barely picked at your tray."

"I ate what you brought me, but what the hospital tried to feed me was dog food. It was worse than dog food. It was roadkill."

He laughed. "At least you ate the chicken soup. Amber said she picked up a few containers and put them in your fridge. Do you want some now?"

"Will it get you to leave me alone?"

"Am I bothering you, Lexie?"

"You're hovering. I don't like it."

"Too bad. I'll be right back. Stay put."

While he was gone, I eased myself off the bed and gripped the edge of my dresser. I wanted to change into something soft and comfortable, but first, I wanted to wash up. My skin was mottled with dried blood, despite the hospital staff's best attempts to sponge it off. More than anything, I wanted to take a shower and wash the entire ordeal away.

I made my way to the bathroom, steeling myself against the dizziness. However, once I pulled the shower curtain open, I wondered if I'd be able to stand long enough to shower.

"Lexie," Michael said from behind, "easy." He realized my intention and turned the water on, plugging the drain. "Let me help."

He snaked an arm around my waist to steady me while he used his other hand to peel the top off of me. He froze at the sight of my bruised torso. It was such a deep purple it was practically black. He swore, squeezing his eyes closed and grinding his teeth. After recomposing himself, his hands went to the zipper on my pants, and I grabbed his wrist.

"I got it," I insisted. "I'm not an invalid." I hated feeling helpless, and I despised the thought of him taking care of me.

"I know you're not, but you have a dozen stitches that can't get wet."

"Stitches?" I brushed my hair out of my face, noticing the bandage wrapped around my forearm. "Dammit."

"It's okay. I'll get the plastic bags and tape, like the nurse showed us."

"You wouldn't let me look when she changed the bandages. Is it that bad?"

Michael pulled me against his chest and hugged me. "It'll be okay."

I didn't like that answer or the tone he used when

he said it. It scared the shit out of me.

Giving up the losing battle, I let Michael take over. He wrapped my bandaged arm in plastic and secured it around my upper arm. After I undressed, he helped me into the tub and washed my hair, making sure not to get the bandage wet and forcing me to keep my arm on the tub ledge. Grabbing the largest, plushest towel he could find, he wrapped it around my body.

"I can take it from here," I said.

"All right. If you need me, call," he insisted, leaving me to get dressed. At least I could dress myself. After pulling on some underwear and an oversized t-shirt, I eased back into bed. "Here," he reappeared while my eyes were closed, "take these and try to eat a little something." I swallowed the two pills and took the offered cup of soup, taking a long sip.

I leaned back against the stack of pillows, hurt, exhausted, and enraged by everything that had happened. Silently, Michael unholstered his gun. He was still dressed for work, and I realized he had never left my side. He had showered in the hospital bathroom, put the same clothes back on, and remained with me the entire time. Taking off the handcuffs, badge, and his button-up shirt, which had my bloodstains on it, he kicked off his shoes and got into bed beside me.

"Thank you for being here. I'm sorry I'm putting you through this," I said.

"Lexie, you didn't do anything wrong. Kemper screwed up." His posture went rigid. "Things like this aren't supposed to happen because your partner should always have your back." He pressed his lips gently against my temple. "You need to get off the street and away from that yahoo who didn't learn a damn thing in the academy."

"It wasn't Kemper's fault."

"I was there when you told Sam and Jack what happened. A third man surprised you, Kemper went after him, and that's when everything went sideways."

"Factually, that's what happened, but you'd have to have been there. Kemper made a judgment call."

"A bad one."

"Let's not talk about this right now. You're making my head hurt." I finished my soup and nestled against Michael, waiting for the constant pain to turn into a dull ache so I could drift off to sleep.

A few hours later, when I opened my eyes, I found Michael sound asleep beside me. I wondered if he'd slept at all over these last few days. I'd never seen him sleep. Every time I woke up, he was always beside me, watching over me. Protecting me. I gave him a hard time about it, but I knew he did it because he loved me, and he'd do the same thing for anyone he cared that deeply about. If it was Sam or Jack or anyone else in his unit, he would have been there for them too.

I didn't want to fault him for that or accuse him of being overprotective. But I wasn't used to anyone taking care of me like this, not even my parents who always had too much on their plates. No one ever would have accused them of being helicopter parents. Sighing, I was glad they were out of town. I didn't want to hear the I told you so.

Reaching for my phone, I sent a text to Amber, thanking her for everything and asking if she could look in on their shop since I was out of commission. She told me she already had and would be by to see me soon. Placing my phone back on the bedside table, I scooted closer to Michael and closed my eyes.

When I awoke again, it was evening. My bed was empty. Michael was gone.

I took a deep breath. Muffled voices carried from the living room and into my bedroom. It took a moment before I realized Amber and Michael were the source of the sound. Taking my time, I got out of bed and went to see what was going on.

"You shouldn't be up. You're supposed to be resting," Amber said.

"What are you doing here?" I asked.

"I told you I was going to stop by. You act like it's a crime to check on my best friend. And after all I did to get you the hunkiest doctors." She winked, her gaze darting briefly in Michael's direction as if to say I could do better. "How are you feeling?"

"Thirsty."

"Water or juice?" She moved toward the fridge, opened the door, and looked inside. "Or do you want a sports drink?"

"Lemon-lime."

She opened the bottle and poured it into a plastic tumbler. "You're so milking this for everything it's worth," she teased.

"Damn straight." I took a seat on the end of the couch, opposite Michael, taking a sip out of the offered cup. "I'm glad you finally got some sleep."

"Same."

"I'll make a dinner run," Amber said. She and Michael exchanged a look. "You can talk while I'm gone." She went to the door. "Trust me, Riley. The sooner, the better."

"What was that about?" I asked, taking another sip before reaching across to put the cup on the coffee table. "Shit." I inhaled, putting my hand up to stop him from rushing to the rescue. "Stretching is a questionable activity. I'd hate to think what sex would be like."

"Lex," he began.

"It was a joke. I don't think either of us is in the mood. Well, maybe you are, but I'm not."

"We need to discuss what happened that night. "

"We already have. I told Preston and Lightman everything. You were in the room. You know what I said."

"I'm not talking about anything official. You can say things to me that you can't say to them."

"Like what? Are you back on the Kemper screwed up kick?"

"He did, but that's not what this is."

"Then what is it?"

"Jack got a hold of some surveillance footage from across the street. The camera had night vision and infrared settings. We can't use it for an ID, but Jack sent me the video anyway. You fought so hard. God." He moved closer, running his fingers across my bruised cheek. "I'm sorry no one came to help. I'm sorry I didn't get there in time."

"Michael," I grasped his hand and brought it to my lips, "I'm okay. Kemper's okay. It doesn't matter."

"It fucking does." He got up to pace.

"I'm right, aren't I?"

He paused mid-stride and turned to face me.

"We can't work together. I'm a distraction. You'll be too worried about me. It'll jeopardize everything."

"Right now, all I want are those assholes' heads on pikes." He blew out a breath. "Tell me everything you remember about them. I don't care if it's the vaguest thing. If the guy reminded you of Richard Nixon, tell me."

"I know I've seen old photos, but off the top of my head, I can't exactly recall what Nixon looks like."

"You know what I mean."

"I told Lightman and Preston everything. The only thing is that tattoo. Is it a gang symbol? Do any members of the Skulls have one?"

"They all have ink. But you never said exactly what

the tattoo looked like. Tell me, Lexie. Please. I want to get a jump on this. I don't want them to hurt anyone else."

"Has someone else been hurt?" It had been three days since Kemper and I were ambushed. Given how rapidly the Skulls escalated from break-ins to murder, more bodies could have turned up in the last seventy-two hours.

"Two more patrol officers were attacked yesterday. Backup arrived to assist, but the assailants got away."

"Did the attack follow the Skulls' MO?"

"To a T. The break-in triggered the alarm, which notified dispatch. When the responding units arrived, they found the spray-painted skull and crown on the wall. Officer Sanchez took a baseball bat to the knee. He'll be out for a while. He'll probably walk with a limp from now on."

"Hawking?"

Michael's brow furrowed. "How did you know he was there?"

"They were working together the last I heard. How is he?"

"He's okay. He fought back. When the second car arrived a minute later, the masked men took off. The backup unit chased them for three blocks before they lost sight of them."

"Did they have another getaway car waiting?"

"A silver SUV. We found it abandoned half a mile away. No prints. The only trace we found was some orange spray paint."

I let the words sink in. "We're looking at two different MOs. The men who came at me and Kemper had guns. No masks. No spray paint. No triggered alarm."

"The trap they set for you outside Cline's jewelry store, in that alley, leads me to believe the Skulls have guns."

"If they do, how come all the attacks, including killing Mr. Cline, were executed with baseball bats and tire irons?"

"They wanted to be quiet. They didn't want to alert anyone else."

"The blaring alarms had done that." A new thought formed in my head. "Unless we're looking at two different teams."

SEVENTEEN

"Do you really think we're looking at two separate teams?" Michael asked.

"It makes sense." I wondered if the offenders were working in tandem. "One group breaks in, tags the place, and makes off with whatever's easy to steal. They trigger the alarm so the police will arrive."

"But the taggers ambushed Officer Cruise. They attacked him."

"With the same tools they used to break into display cases and force the cash drawer open."

Michael considered my words. "The men who set a trap in that alleyway near Cline's store were waiting for you. They weren't trying to escape."

"And they tried to shoot Kemper." I stared at Michael, worried how he'd react to the next words out of my mouth. "Why didn't they shoot me? I was an easier target. I wasn't protected. I got wrapped up in a freaking tarp. No protection. No idea what was going on. Kemper was inside a metal dumpster. They couldn't know if they'd hit him or not."

"It was scare tactics," Michael said. "We were supposed to catch on. They wanted us to know how close they could get."

"But we were too stupid to figure it out."

"You figured it out that next night."

"We would have figured it out sooner if the gunshot had sounded like a gunshot."

"When they analyzed the bullet, they found melted plastic fused to it, along with cotton fibers. We can't know for certain, but we've seen some homemade suppressors made with coke bottles and balled up towels. I'm guessing that's why the shot didn't sound like a shot."

"I knew it."

Michael smiled. "Detective chops."

"Unfortunately, I don't see how any of this helps us." I slumped back against the couch cushion. "These are theories. We have nothing to support them."

"Not yet, but that could change. If we are looking at two teams, we need to prepare. The men breaking in and spray painting the Skulls' symbol could be nothing more than bait or a distraction. The second team poses the most risk."

"Except for Mr. Cline. He wasn't shot, Michael. He was bludgeoned. How does that fit into any of this?"

"It fits if they are working together. The Skulls' numbers may have dwindled after we made sweeping arrests, but they still have more than a dozen foot soldiers looking to start a war."

I closed my eyes, desperate to recall more from the ambush at the liquor store. In a lot of ways, it was similar to the alley in that the men lured us into a trap. "Can you get photos of the men Kemper and I spoke to outside the sex shop? The ones Lightman followed that night."

"Yeah, but—"

"Preston doesn't want me to see them before I speak to a sketch artist. She's afraid it'll confuse my memory." Unfortunately, she wasn't wrong. Witnesses created false memories all the time. And while police were trained to be more vigilant and aware, we were still human. "The head injury won't help matters, especially if a defense attorney wants to pick things apart."

"First, we need to identify these guys and stop them. Court proceedings aren't our problem. Getting these assholes off the street is, especially when they are targeting our own."

"You said Sanchez and Hawking got jumped when responding to another call. But the men who attacked them were responsible for the break-in."

"That's what they both said. They had the gas masks on and had the spray paint with them."

"And they used club-like weapons. No guns."

"What are you thinking, Lexie?"

"Where was the second team? If the two are working together, why didn't the second group, the assholes with the guns, intervene? Sanchez was down for the count. It was just Hawking and the two offenders. If the gunmen stepped in, they could have..." I reached for the bottle and took a sip of the neon yellow liquid. I didn't want to put the words out there. Murdering any cop was bad, but one who I considered a friend was even worse.

"That attack happened after you and Kemper fought them in the liquor store. It was two nights later." Michael glanced at the clock on my wall. "You got a piece of them. They may be holed up somewhere, licking their wounds."

"A broken nose wouldn't put anyone out of commission," I said.

"You told me you thought you shot one."

"I said I wasn't sure."

"Maybe you did. Hospitals and emergency care centers have been notified to keep an eye out."

"They didn't need the reminder. Gunshot wounds

always get reported."

Michael gave me a look.

"Almost always," I said. "There are always exceptions and underhanded practices, money under the table, and things like that, but a hospital or doctor's office has too many healthcare providers and too many witnesses. Someone would say something."

"Which is why we're also keeping an eye on veterinarian offices, places that perform cosmetic procedures, and all the back alley doctors we know about."

"There must be dozens."

"Maybe hundreds." Michael drummed his fingers against his thigh. "As soon as Amber gets back with dinner, I'll head to the station and see if there have been any recent developments. I'll share our theory with Jack and see what he has to say. Frank's been working every informant he has for intel, but no one's talking about this."

"It's gang business. Does he have an in with the Skulls?"

"Not since we made that big bust. After that, no one's talking to anyone."

"So he did have someone on the inside."

Michael shook his head. "Not really. We have a lot of friendlies in a lot of places, but what they would share with us is only what would hurt their competition, not their own."

I thought about what Michael had said. "What about going to their rivals?"

"Whatever the Skulls have planned, they haven't talked about. Usually, groups like that run their mouths to prove how big and bad they are. Killing cops or threatening to kill cops is usually a good way to get promoted to the top of the food chain."

"Like a lot of old school rap music?"

"Pretty much."

"I didn't realize this was Compton."

"We aren't that far away," Michael pointed out.

"Decades," I said. I liked to believe things had changed for the better for those communities, but most of the time, it didn't feel like it. "So we can't go to the Skulls' rivals for intel, and no one inside the Skulls is talking. All we know is we're public enemy number one."

"Still with the rap analogy?" Michael teased.

I shook my head, realizing there was something else that I had missed. "Shit."

"What?" He moved toward me, concerned.

"What are you doing here?"

He froze, confused. "What?"

"You've been with me since the liquor store. You never left my side."

"That's not entirely true."

"You stayed in the hospital with me. You brought me home. You've been here all day. Oh god." The look Preston had given him came to mind. "Why haven't you been at work?"

"You don't think this is where I should be?" The hurt look in his eyes made me cringe. "You think there's something more important I should be doing?"

"That's not what I meant. But you didn't stay with Cruise when he got hurt. You're not checking in on Sanchez."

"We worked closely together, Lexie. It's different."

"They know."

"It doesn't matter if they do. But they don't," he insisted. "Jack and Sam told me to stay with you. They wanted to know everything that happened. I spoke to Kemper. I took his statement. I went over all of this with him at the hospital. And I went over it again with you. I've been working. As far as Jack is concerned,

I've been doing my job. And as far as I'm concerned, making sure you're okay is my only job." He brushed my hair out of my face. It had gotten a little out of control after my nap. "Relax, honey. Our secret's safe for now."

"Preston knows. She's known for a while."

"And she'll cover for me. It's no big deal." He gave me a lopsided smile. "Don't you think we have more important things going on than to worry about sneaking around behind the brass's back?"

"I don't want this to bite us in the ass on top of everything else."

"It won't. That's the one thing I can promise you." He pressed his lips to my forehead. "How are you feeling?"

"Better now." I stared down at the bandage on my arm. "But I'd like to do something useful."

"I thought you'd say that." Michael climbed off the couch and came back with his notepad and a few folders. I didn't remember seeing them before, but he must have had them with him at the hospital. "Here. This is Kemper's account. Tell me if he left anything out. I don't trust that guy not to cover his own ass."

I read Kemper's report. From what I could tell, he was taking the blame for what happened. "This reads like I remember." I pointed to the bottom of the page. "I can't be sure about any of this though. I was inside. Kemper was half out the door. He could see into the parking lot. I couldn't."

"I wish I'd been there to protect you," Michael said quietly.

"That's not your job."

"No, that was your partner's job." He kissed my shoulder. "I'm your partner off the job, so I should have done something to stop these bastards before things got to this point. They've been committing these crimes for two weeks, but we never sounded the alarm until it was too late. Maybe if gangs had warned the rest of the department, we would have determined their identities and arrested these assholes by now. I never should have taken you with me to Cline's jewelry store. Maybe if I hadn't, none of this would have happened."

"We don't even know if that has anything to do with this. We're assuming these crimes are connected, that two groups of men are working together to hurt cops, but it's just a theory. Our theory. And even if they are connected, there's no way they would have known who would respond to the liquor store break-in." A flash of something important ran through my mind, but it was gone before I could latch on to it.

"You're just saying that to make me feel better."

"I said it because it's the truth." I skimmed Kemper's statement again. "Did the convenience store owner ever talk to a sketch artist?"

"What convenience store owner?"

I pointed to the notes Michael had hastily scrawled at the top of the page. Our first call that night was barely worth noting. But it kept us in the neighborhood, and if these bastards were into setting traps, the convenience store could have been bait. "You should speak to the owner. The security camera didn't work, but he got a look at the three men who ransacked his store. I suggested he speak to a sketch artist, but he kept going on about how they were hooligans with baggy jeans and," I squeezed my eyes shut, shaking my head, "something. There's something I'm forgetting."

"It's okay. Kemper was there too. Unless he abandoned you at that crime scene, he should be able to fill-in whatever memory gaps you may have."

"I don't want memory gaps," I snapped.

Michael held up his palms. "I know, but you heard what the doctor said. Things may be a little spotty from that night. It shouldn't be permanent, but you did sustain a pretty serious knock to the noggin'." Michael thought about what I'd said. "Three men broke into the convenience store. And three men were waiting for you and Kemper inside the liquor store. Do you think they could be the same men?"

"I don't know. The store owner made them sound like kids."

"How old was he?" Michael asked.

"I don't know. Why does that matter?"

"It could be why he called them kids and why you and Kemper called them men."

I flipped to another page, skimming the details surrounding the condition of the liquor store when the backup unit arrived. At the very end of the report were photos from the crime scene. Kemper had been wedged between the broken doorframe. I'd been a few inches away, sprawled out inside the shop. Blood covered a lot of the tiles, pooling in places and leaving lots of smears. Scrawled on the floor in the blood were the words, *Screw with us again, and see what happens.*

My forearm ached, and I remembered Michael pressing down against it and Preston asking a question when the EMTs were working on me. "One of those bastards carved something into my arm, didn't he? A message? A warning? Something?" I pulled at the tape holding the bandage in place.

"Lexie," Michael's hand shook as he gently pulled my other hand away from the wound, "leave it be for now."

I met his eyes, seeing rage burning deep within their depths. He'd kill the sons of a bitch. I had no doubt. "What did they do?"

"It doesn't matter. It'll heal. Amber knows several good plastic surgeons on staff. They did the stitches. They'll make it go away. It'll be like it never happened."

His words only frightened me more, and I frantically pulled the bandage off. The knife wounds had been stitched and glued to the point I could barely make out the message, *You're Mine.*

EIGHTEEN

I pressed the tape back in place, sickened at the sight. No wonder Michael wanted to kill them. So did I.

"They'll pay for this, Lex. I promise."

How dare they? It was the only thought that played through my head. The self-doubt and blame had taken a back seat. Some asshole did this because he thought he could, but he'd face the consequences. I wouldn't let this go until he was behind bars. "We have to figure out who they are."

"We will." Michael pried the folder out of my shaking hands.

"We can't let them do this to someone else. They attacked Cruise, killed Mr. Cline, hurt Sanchez, and they tried to kill me and Kemper. We have to stop them."

"They're not going to get the chance to do this to anyone because I'm going to find them." His words were so cold and measured, I believed he meant it. "I need to write down everything you remember. I'll bring it to Jack tonight, and we'll get started on it. Tomorrow, you'll sit with the sketch artist and see what's what."

"What about Kemper? Did he sit with a sketch artist?"

Michael nodded, but the look on his face told me he wasn't pleased with the results.

"Promise me something first," I said. "Promise me you are not going to go after these guys on your own."

"Lexie—"

"Promise me, or I'll call Preston and fill her in on the situation instead."

"You'd call Sam?"

"I don't know everything that happened between the two of you, and I don't want to know. But she cares a great deal about you, and she wants you to be safe and happy. If anyone in gangs can protect you from yourself, it's her."

"She's my ex."

"Exactly, which is how she knows there's something going on between the two of us. She picked up on it faster than anyone else, despite your best attempts."

Michael looked more annoyed. "Did she say something to you?"

"After we closed that last case, she told me not to hurt you."

"Why didn't you say something before now?"

"I did. Now, stop trying to change the subject." I yawned, moving the pillow around so I could lie down. "Either promise me you aren't going to do something that will jeopardize this case or your integrity, or hand me the phone." I pointed to the cell phone sitting on the table. "Those are your only options."

"Do you really think you're in a position to negotiate?"

"I shouldn't have to. You said I could trust you. That we are partners. I need to know you have my back and you'll do things the right way. If you can't, then we'll never be able to work together."

"We can work together," he said indignantly. "At

the moment, I'd like nothing more." He grabbed a pen and paper. "I promise I won't go after them on my own. Now can we begin?"

"Let's do this."

~*~

The next morning, loud banging sounded at my front door. I rolled over, surprised to find Michael in bed beside me. After Amber showed up with dinner, Michael had made himself scarce. He told me not to expect to see him again, that he planned to work through the night and would crash at his own apartment so he could get a change of clothes and take care of a few things. So what was he doing here?

The banging at the door caused him to shift, and he reached for his gun. "Are you expecting company?" he asked.

"I wasn't even expecting you."

"Okay." He blinked, staring bleary-eyed at the clock. "Stay here. I'll see what's going on."

"You can't go to the door with a gun."

"You want to bet?" He wasn't fooling around. He really thought someone was knocking on my door to finish what they started a few nights ago.

The medication from the night before had worn off, and my headache was back with a vengeance. I felt worse this morning than I did last night. In fact, I felt a little sick.

Michael left my room and continued to the front door. Quickly, I opened my nightstand drawer, unlocked the gun safe, and pulled out my off duty piece. I hadn't seen my service piece since the liquor store. It must have been confiscated, but I hadn't even thought about it until now. Maybe it was because I didn't realize I needed it.

The pounding stopped, and I strained to hear what was going on while I sat up in bed, resting my arms on top of my bent knees and aiming toward the door.

"What are you doing here? Where's Lexie?" Kemper asked.

"You son of a bitch," Michael snarled loud enough that I heard him through the closed bedroom door. "What the hell were you thinking?"

I put the gun on the nightstand and lunged forward. The room spun, and I thought I might hurl. Shouldn't the worst be over by now? But I didn't have time to wait for things to settle.

"I wasn't," Kemper replied. "I didn't think—"

"That's right, you didn't think." A loud bang reverberated against the thin walls of my apartment and inside my skull. "Don't you ever do anything that stupid again." The noise sounded again. "Do you understand me?"

"I just want to see Lexie and make sure she's okay."

"She's not okay, you piece of shit. Do you have any idea what could have happened? It's bad, but it could have been much worse. If I hadn't gotten there when I did, she could have bled out. Do you understand that?"

"Let me talk to her. I need to apologize."

"What you need is for someone to knock you upside your freaking head with a bottle and see how you like it, but you'd be too stupid to remember this conversation ever happened."

I needed to get to the living room before Michael killed Kemper. Opening the bedroom door, I made it to the end of the hallway, clinging to the wall. Michael had Kemper pinned against the door. I wasn't sure if Kemper was too afraid to move or Michael wouldn't let him. Michael's hands were on Kemper's shoulders, pressing him into the wall.

"Michael, stop," I said, but his hands didn't loosen. "Riley, let him go. Now," I snapped, loud enough that the sound of my own voice practically brought me to my knees.

Michael released him, and Kemper gasped. "Lexie," they both said at once.

"Detective Riley, back off." I white-knuckled the corner of the wall to remain upright.

"Lexie," Kemper looked at me with pity in his eyes, "I didn't realize they'd get the jump on you. I just reacted."

"It's okay. We survived." I stared at the way he cradled his left side. "Are you okay?"

"I'm fine."

Michael almost opened his mouth, but one look from me kept him from uttering a word.

"I came as soon as I heard you were released from the hospital. I wanted to check on you and see how you were. I brought flowers." Kemper pointed to a pathetic bouquet that had fallen to the floor. He scooped it up and put it on the side table, not making a move to come any closer for fear Michael would intervene. "I heard you were going to talk to the sketch artist today. I told him what I could the day after it happened, but it was so dark in there. I didn't see much."

"I know."

Kemper glanced at Michael. "I didn't realize you were going over things with Lexie here." He looked back at me. "I thought you'd be going to the station. I wanted to offer to take you to breakfast and give you a ride. I guess I should have called first." Kemper quirked an eyebrow at my pajama pants, his thoughts concerning our level of undress obvious. And he wasn't wrong.

"You should have called," Michael said.

"Next time." Kemper backed toward the door. "Is there anything I can do?"

"Just go," Michael said.

"Lexie?" Kemper asked.

"We need to catch these guys. If you remember anything else, say something."

"I will, but I've already answered everyone's questions. I don't think I'm forgetting anything."

"What about the convenience store?" I turned to Michael. "We were discussing that. The store owner said three kids were responsible. Three men attacked us."

"You really think it was the same crew?" Kemper asked. "It didn't sound like it."

"We're exploring every possibility," Michael said gruffly.

"But we didn't see them. The cameras didn't work. We have no way of knowing anything about them. The store owner only gave the vaguest description," Kemper said.

"See?" I looked at Michael. "I told you that."

Michael rubbed a hand over his face. "Yeah, which is why Jack and I spoke to him last night."

"I thought you just asked about that this morning," Kemper said.

Michael growled, moving a few inches closer. "It's time for you to leave."

"I'm not going anywhere until I make this right with Lexie." Kemper showed more bravery than I imagined. "Do you want me to leave, Lex?"

Shit. He knew. He had his proof, and he could use it to destroy whatever chances I still had at detective. Though, given everything that happened, I wasn't sure either of us would pass the exam.

"Bobby, please don't say anything."

"I won't, but I hope you know what you're doing."

He gave Michael an uncertain look. "Guess this explains a lot."

Michael lunged for him.

"Stop." I grabbed Michael's shoulder before he could put his hands on Kemper. "Check on Hawking and Sanchez and see how they are. Text me and let me know, okay?"

Kemper gave Michael an uncertain look. "Yeah, okay. Call if you need anything. Day or night. I don't care. I won't let you down again."

"You need to leave now," Michael insisted, stepping closer to the door. "She's heard your apology, and she's asked you to do something. Go do it. And don't come back unless you're invited. Lexie's supposed to avoid loud sounds and stress."

It looked like Kemper was about to point out the obvious flaw in Michael's logic, but he let it go, gave me another contrite look, and went out the door, closing it as gently as possible behind him.

"Do you believe that guy?" Michael snorted. "He thinks he can show up, say he's sorry, and that'll fix things."

"Shit. He knows. Shit. Shit. Shit." I leaned my back against the wall, needing the extra support. "You acted like an animal staking his claim. What is wrong with you?"

"Calm down."

"If you wanted me calm, you should have thought about that before you started acting like some alpha male Neanderthal. For all I know, he's going to report you for threatening him." A sharp pain shot through me, and Michael wrapped his arms around me before my knees buckled.

"I'm sorry."

"Sorry? You just said sorry was pointless, and it doesn't fix anything."

"Lex," he faltered, "I am sorry."

"That we got caught or that I didn't let you pummel Kemper?"

Another sharp pain shot through me. This time, it started behind my eyes and it didn't go away. Damn migraines. The doctor said the concussion would make them more likely. I gasped, tears rolling down my cheeks, my entire body shaking from the stress and pain.

Michael lowered us onto the floor. "Are you okay?"

"No." I pressed against Michael's chest, hoping to get myself under control, but only after my head pounded in time to my heartbeat and my vision blurred did the sharp pain quiet. As everything dimmed, Michael carried me back to the bedroom, pulled the covers up around me, and held me tight.

"Talk to me, Lexie. Can you breathe? Can you see? You could have a brain bleed." He peered into each of my eyes, checking to see if I had blown a pupil.

"Stop that." I swatted at his hand. "It's just a migraine from all this damn drama."

He leaned over me, tucking my hair behind my ears and carefully assessing me. "Are you sure you're okay? I'd feel better if someone at the ER checks you out."

"I just need someplace dark and quiet."

"All right, but if it gets worse, you better say something."

"Haven't you made enough threats today?"

Michael pressed his lips gently to my temple before getting out of bed and closing the blinds and adjusting the thermostat to make it cooler. Then he slid beneath the covers and held me.

The next time I opened my eyes, it was noon. "Michael," I whispered, afraid the timbre of my own voice would be too loud in my ears, "tell me none of that happened."

"I can't, and I'm not apologizing again. You have to see it from my perspective. Those men could have killed you. When I saw Kemper's stupid face, the only thing I could think of was how close I almost came to losing you."

"You didn't lose me."

"I should have never taken you to Cline's."

"It's not your fault. It's not Kemper's either."

"Your breakdown a few nights ago in my apartment was my fault. This morning, your migraine, that's also my fault, just like our secret getting out."

"It didn't get out. Kemper won't say anything, but you can't antagonize him. Promise me you won't."

Michael took an unsteady breath. "Okay." He pressed his lips to mine. "Is there anything else?"

"I don't like it when you get aggressive like that. The man I saw in my living room scares me."

"I hope you know I would never hurt you."

"I know, but I won't be with someone who uses violence to solve his problems. I don't want you hurting anyone."

"That's a little hard to do. I'm a cop."

"That's different. That's work, and there are rules and ethics to follow. Plus, you always say you separate your work life from your private life." I winced, and he focused his eyes on the light peeking through the side of the drapes.

"Is that bothering you?" he asked.

"Almost as much as you threatening Kemper." I closed my eyes and dropped his hand. "Let's not fight. I can't do this right now."

"No, we're done. It won't happen again."

After securing the drapes so no light could invade the sanctity of my bedroom, Michael went into the kitchen and came back with four pieces of lightly buttered toast, a glass of orange juice, and two pills.

I downed the pills first before working my way through three pieces of toast. It wasn't much, but eating wasn't a priority. Once I finished breakfast, I crawled out of bed. It was time I got back to work.

NINETEEN

The sketch artist clicked the mouse a few more times. "Like this?"

"Just like that," I said.

"Any idea what it might be?" Michael asked.

"It could be anything." The sketch artist moved back to the man's face. "Do you recall any other features?"

"That's it. Lots of dark. Lots of shadows." I studied the photo on the screen. The details I provided led to a rather plain sketch. The tattoo was the only thing that stuck out in my mind. Other than that, the men who attacked me looked like just about anyone.

"Flashlight beams wash everything out." The sketch artist saved the image and printed a copy. "Wrinkles, scars, other imperfections, and the dark conceals everything in shadow. It was a bad combination. You're lucky to have seen as much as you did." He said it to make me feel better, but it wasn't working.

"What did Kemper come up with?"

He opened another file. "His isn't that different from yours, except his version makes the men inside the liquor store look a little more like super villains from one of those Frank Miller movies."

I didn't understand the reference, but it didn't

matter.

"Are you just about finished?" Detective Lightman asked, joining us at Michael's desk where the sketch artist had set up shop.

Michael handed Lightman the hard copy. "Running down that tattoo is our best bet."

Lightman shrugged. "Fine. You want to do it. Go do it."

Michael nodded, cast one last look in my direction, and headed for the double doors.

"C'mon, Sarconi," Lightman jerked his head toward the conference room, "we have everything waiting for you."

Getting up, I followed Lightman across the bullpen. He opened the door, holding it for me. Inside, I spotted Lt. Peterson, Detective Preston, and another detective I didn't recognize waiting.

"Thanks for coming in," Preston said. "How are you feeling?"

"Like I wish I could do more."

Peterson gestured to one of the seats and waited for me to sit down. "It's been days since the incident. Normally, I'd speak to an injured officer as soon as possible, but Detective Riley took care of that. You spoke to him at the scene and several times while you were in the hospital, and once since you've been released. We need you to go over this information again. You're not in any trouble, Sarconi. It's just procedure."

The detective I didn't recognize kept his mouth shut. He didn't introduce himself or offer an explanation as to why he was sitting in on this meeting, but I didn't like the way he was watching me, as if he expected to catch me in a lie.

"Where should I begin?"

"When you arrived at the liquor store." Peterson

picked up his pen and scanned the statement in front of him.

I went over all the details again. For what felt like the hundredth time, I explained what happened during my last shift. The convenience store. The liquor store. Kemper chasing the third suspect. At this point, it sounded rehearsed, but I didn't care.

Lt. Peterson made a few notations. The other detective asked another dozen questions about Kemper's attitude and actions. That's when I realized he must work for internal affairs.

"What was Kemper's frame of mind?" he asked.

"I couldn't say."

"You spent your entire shift with him. You've been riding together for quite some time. Surely, you must have known how he was feeling, what he was thinking about, if anything was bothering him, if he had reasons to be distracted." It sounded like he wanted to throw my partner under the bus, but I wasn't cooperating.

"As far as I know, he was focused on work. We'd been given specific instructions before we rolled out that night to request backup and keep an eye out. If anything, we were a little on edge. More alert."

"And yet, neither of you noticed a third offender inside the liquor store."

"It was too dark to see. The lights weren't on. We did the best we could." I spotted Michael lingering outside the conference room. He pretended to be busy, but I suspected he was listening to every word. "If this is punitive, I have a right to have my union rep here."

"No one's in any trouble, Sarconi," Peterson assured me. "We're just trying to figure out where this guy was hiding and how these three men got the jump on two trained and decorated officers."

"Like I said, it was dark. We couldn't see. As soon as we spotted the third man, Kemper attempted to apprehend him."

"Which left you vulnerable and open to attack by the other two offenders," the IA investigator said.

"It was a mistake. Kemper wouldn't intentionally put a fellow officer at risk. So much happened so quickly. Backup was en route. They should have shown up sooner. If they had, we wouldn't have been outnumbered. We wouldn't have gotten surprised."

"Why didn't you wait for backup?"

"That's enough," Lightman said. "Sarconi knew the stakes. So did Officer Kemper. They couldn't wait. That's not what we do. That would go against your precious protocol."

"I think I have heard more than enough." The IA investigator stood. "I'd like to apologize that you were placed in that position, Officer Sarconi. I'm glad you're okay."

"Thanks." I tried to keep the bitterness and annoyance out of my voice. Kemper made a bad call, but it wasn't intentional. I wasn't sure what the right call would have been. If the two other men hadn't taken advantage and Kemper hadn't gotten jumped by the third guy, maybe it would have been the right call. Now I was second-guessing everything. Leaning back in the chair, I asked, "Are we done? I'm getting a headache."

"We're done." Lt. Peterson patted my shoulder. "I expect you to make a full recovery and be back at work as soon as possible. These bastards can't keep benching our best officers." He went to the door. "Detective Lightman mentioned you were hoping to assist gangs on the case before you were attacked. Whenever you get back, I'll make sure there's a desk waiting for you here."

"Thank you, sir."

"Thanks, Lieutenant," Lightman said. "Sarconi has proven herself to be an asset on more than one occasion. We could use more like her."

Once the lieutenant was gone, Lightman dropped into the chair he vacated.

"Jack, go easy," Preston warned. "Give Sarconi some room to breathe. She's not feeling well."

"Are you all right? Do you want to go home?" The way Lightman asked those questions sounded more like a test than actual concern.

"What do you need, sir?"

"That's what I like to hear."

Preston glanced out the door, catching a glimpse of Michael. Her lips pressed into a tight line. When Michael looked in her direction, she shook her head, but Lightman was too focused on me to notice their exchange.

Lightman gave me a look. "Okay, it's time you talk to us."

"I already spilled my guts. What more can I possibly say?"

"We aren't looking to place blame or hand out reprimands. You're one of five officers who has seen these assholes in person," Lightman said. "Cruise didn't get a look at them, and he's gonna be out for several weeks. Kemper's guilty conscience has impaired his ability to function. He can't seem to find his way out of a paper bag. Hawking only saw the gas mask, nothing more. Same with Sanchez, so that makes you our best bet."

"That's a pretty pathetic bet," I said before thinking to censor my retort.

Preston took over before Lightman could jump on my case. "You keep saying you've seen the tattoo before, but you haven't given us much to go on."

Preston pulled a photo out of a folder and slid it across the table. "Is that the tattoo?"

It was a blown-up image of the neck tattoo. "That's it." I traced my finger around the spiked edges of the ink. "Is that a letter?"

"We think it's this." Preston slid a photo of the spray-painted skull and crown tag toward me.

"Shit."

"You said the men outside the sex shop were up to no good. It looks like you were right," Lightman said.

"Why didn't you arrest them? I thought you checked into them and determined they weren't involved in this case."

"So you're looking to pass blame?" Lightman's eyebrows went skyward. "You think this is somehow my fault?"

"No, sir. However, I don't know what else I can say. I reported them to you. When I returned from shift, they had filed a complaint against me. I don't know what I'm supposed to think."

"That complaint was bogus," Preston said. "Everyone knows that. Don't worry. It won't sully your record."

"That's not—" I stopped. There was no point in arguing, especially when my head really did hurt.

"The men you reported aren't known members of the Skulls," Lightman said. "They don't have any official connections or ties to the gang. However, the tattoo may be a sign of gang loyalty or a brand of some sort."

"Like an initiation?" I asked.

"Not exactly. We believe the tattoo is a marking saying they are under the gang's protection. Others have the same mark."

"How does that work?" I asked. "Flying colors is usually why people get killed."

"But no other gang will look to recruit them. We think the Skulls started doing this to keep their family together. Sometimes, the guys in the life don't want their little brothers or cousins getting mixed up in things. So the tattoo marked them as off limits. They pledged their loyalty, but they never became active members."

It sounded ridiculous, but I didn't know all the rules of the street. "So the men outside the sex shop and one of the men from inside the liquor store have ties to the Skulls without being directly connected to what's going on?"

"We think with their decimated ranks and the war the Skulls declared on the police, that these," Lightman struggled to come up with a proper term, "gang reserves are stepping up to the plate. Most of them don't have records. They've stayed off our radar, so we don't know who they are. We can make a few guesses, but it's unsubstantiated conjecture. That's why I want you to go through every known member of the Skulls' family tree. Maybe you'll recognize someone."

"What happened with the convenience store?" I asked. "The owner or clerk, whatever he was, said three men ransacked the place and ripped off the register. Could they be the same men Kemper and I encountered at the liquor store later that night?"

Lightman chuckled. "Mike didn't tell you?"

Kemper's appearance at my apartment prevented that from happening. "No, sir."

"He should have. You were right. The convenience store owner said one of those little shits had a tattoo on his neck too. We're guessing it's the same group of men."

"In that case, he's your best bet for a positive ID. The three men were inside his store. The lights were on. They were in plain sight. He confronted two of them. He has to know what they look like."

"He's given a few different renditions of the perps to the sketch artist. We released the compilations over the wire." Lightman reached into his jacket pocket and pulled out a few folded sheets of paper. "You saw these men up close and personal. Tell me if these pictures match what you remember."

He laid them flat on the table in front of me. I picked up the closest one. It looked so generic. The emphasis was on the baggy clothing, not on the men's faces.

"They're not kids. The store owner kept saying they were snot-nosed punks, but they're men, early to mid-twenties. I can't tell you what they were wearing, aside from the fact that at least one of them had a belt. They were in jeans. I don't remember them being excessively baggie or skinny."

"The pants, not the men?" Preston asked.

"Yeah, the pants."

"Anything else?" Preston grabbed a bottle of water off the back table and held it out to me. "Do you want one?"

"No."

But she put it on the table in front of me anyway. I glanced out the door, wondering if Michael had used some sort of telepathy to encourage her to get me something to drink. But I didn't see him lingering nearby.

"How did you make the connection between the convenience store and the liquor store?" Lightman asked.

"There were three guys at both scenes. The two crimes occurred near the same neighborhood and within a reasonable timeframe. It makes sense it could be the same crew, especially since someone has been trying to lure cops into a trap."

"We heard rumblings from a few CIs that the Skulls have been keeping their eyes peeled for signs of police activity. Even if we respond to a call they didn't create, they may still try to use it to their advantage to trap us. They want to hit us where it hurts. We were getting too close to identifying them, so they switched from defense to offense to throw us off our game and off their scent," Preston said.

"What do you mean?" I asked.

"This morning, another jewelry store was robbed." Lightman collected the sketches and stuffed them inside a folder. "No one else has been killed yet, but the thieves went back to eliminate Cline after the fact. So the most recent victim didn't even want to file a report. He's afraid what they'll do to him if they think he's assisting our investigation. He said the alarm was accidentally tripped, but I saw the destroyed display cases. It's his word against ours, and unless he wants to report a crime, we can't investigate. Our hands are tied. We need you to come up with something. You saw them. You fought them. You nearly arrested them."

"I don't know who they are."

"Then help us figure it out."

TWENTY

I squinted, massaging my throbbing temples. "I don't know. What about speaking to the two men Kemper and I rousted? They have the same tattoo. Put them in the box and make them talk."

"On what grounds?" Preston asked. "They were loitering outside a shop. You told them to move it along, and they did. After which, they filed a harassment complaint against you. There's not much we can do to persuade them to cooperate."

Resting my head in my hands, I closed my eyes. My skull threatened to split open. And I thought the migraines I used to get were bad.

I'd spent the last hour flipping through mugshots of men with tattoos on their necks. Most didn't have the skull and crown tattoo, but since we couldn't be certain that was the ink I'd seen, Lightman wanted me to rule out the other possibilities. I didn't recognize anyone.

My face felt hot, the rest of me cold. If I turned my head too fast, I'd get sick. Why couldn't I remember better? Those three men nearly killed Kemper and me.

"The convenience store owner needs a protection detail," I said, my mind back on the night of the attack.

"Already done." Preston pushed away from the table. Lightman had left us alone when watching me flip through photos became too tedious. "Come on, let me take you home."

"I'm fine."

"You look like you're about to pass out."

"Yeah, okay." Slowly, I stood, swallowing to keep the bile down. "I didn't drive myself here."

"I know." She opened the conference room door and held it for me. "I'll give you a ride."

We didn't speak on the drive back to my apartment, which was a relief since I had to focus on keeping my stomach contents in my stomach. Pressing my forehead against the cold glass of the window helped. So did Preston's careful driving.

She followed me upstairs and came into my apartment. I dropped onto the couch, wondering if Michael had left anything incriminating behind but in too much discomfort to give it much thought. Preston knew we were together. What would be the point of hiding it?

Spotting my pill bottles on the counter, she picked them up and gave the pain meds a shake. "When's the last time you took one of these?"

"When I woke up this morning."

"Do you need another one?" She read the label. "It says every six hours. I think you're past due."

"They make me sleepy. But I'll take one anyway."

She brought it to me with a glass of water. "Is it your head or your arm?"

"Right now, my head." I took a small sip, enough to get the pill down, and put the glass on the coffee table, which reminded me my middle didn't feel so great either. "Did you see the footage?"

"The infrared? Yeah, I saw it."

I stared at the bandages on my arm. "Why would they do this?"

"Be thankful they didn't do something worse. Something more permanent."

"More permanent than carving a message into my arm?"

"Scars suck, Sarconi. I won't lie to you about that. But the psychological ones suck worse. They could have done anything they wanted to you that night. It might not seem like it, but you got off easy." She shook her head. "That didn't come out right. What I'm trying to say—"

"I know what you're trying to say. And you're right. Kemper and I both got lucky. If backup wasn't on the way, if his vest hadn't stopped the bullet..." I wanted to cry. I hadn't since the attack, but suddenly, it all felt like too much. Picking up the glass, I took another small sip. The cool water calmed the inner turmoil.

Preston moved around my kitchen, spotting one of the flower arrangements. "Who sent this one?"

"Kemper," I said, thankful for the distraction.

"There are only two good things about getting hurt on the job, paid sick leave and the swag you get from everyone at the station. When you get back, it'll be free lunch and drinks for the first week. After that, everything will go back to normal."

"I can't even remember what normal feels like."

Preston took a seat beside me. "How's Michael holding up?"

"I don't know." I looked toward the wall where he had pinned Kemper only hours earlier, wondering if there were telltale cracks or blemishes in the paint. "Did Kemper say something?"

Preston gave me a confused look. "Why would Kemper say something?"

"Never mind." The last thing I wanted was to get

Michael in trouble.

"Mike blames him for what happened to you. He's always been wary of him. I'd say he has reason. Kemper wasn't exactly subtle with his feelings."

"Kemper isn't interested in me any more than he's interested in anyone else." I snorted. "In fact, I'd say he's pretty interested in you." Which made me wonder if that was another reason Michael loathed him.

She didn't say anything at first. Instead, she looked around my apartment. "Mike wouldn't want you to be here alone. He's worried about you. Terrified. He knows what the job entails, but he's never faced the possibility of losing someone he cares this much about until now. It's one thing to risk himself. It's something else to see it happen to someone he loves. The helplessness would tear anyone up inside." From her tone, I knew she was speaking from personal experience, but we weren't close enough for me to ask about it. "That's how he's felt since we responded to your radio call for backup."

"Does Lightman know?"

"About the two of you?" Preston shook her head. "Jack's a great detective, but he's been too distracted to catch on yet. I don't know how much longer that will last, but for now, he's willing to turn a blind eye and ignore what's in front of him."

"Are we that obvious?"

"No," she said. "But Michael's part of our team. We don't usually keep secrets from one another."

"What about Peterson or that detective from IA who questioned me?"

"No one knows, except me. And I'm the last person who would ever say anything about your relationship."

"We're waiting until after the detective's exam before we disclose, if I still take it."

"That's a wise decision." Her phone chimed, and she read the message. "I should head back. Michael's on his way. But Sarconi, you definitely should take the exam."

Once I was sure she was gone, I climbed into bed. How could I help when I couldn't even last an entire afternoon?

A few minutes later, my front door opened. "Lexie," Michael called softly, "it's me."

"Did you hear what happened?" I asked, not believing he hadn't been eavesdropping on what was going on inside the conference room.

He came into my bedroom. "The brass wants to bury Kemper for screwing up. No surprise there."

"What about the rest?" I met his eyes, but he looked confused. "Didn't Lightman tell you what he thinks the tattoo is actually of?"

"Yes." He sat down at the end of my bed. "But it's a long-shot. I was going to tell you this morning, but we were interrupted."

"I really thought things would have gone better with the sketch artist. It's my fault. I thought we'd get an ID. Instead, we still have nothing."

"Not nothing. We have three different sets of sketches. We'll put them together and see what we get."

"Why can't I remember things more clearly? When I think about that night, all I see is the gun aimed at Kemper. And the weapon discharging." My chin trembled. "And the sound."

He crawled up the bed toward me. "Hey," he gently grasped my face, "look at me. Tell me what you remember, however you remember it. Start with the gun."

"It was a Glock 17 with a stainless slide. The light kept reflecting off it. At first, I thought the whole thing was silver because he wore black gloves, but it was just the slide." In my mind, the weapon discharged in slow-motion like in those stylized action films.

"That's great, Lex." He pressed his lips to my forehead. "What else?"

"Nothing."

"Come on, think."

"He had cold eyes. Dark. Almost entirely black. That was the man who grabbed me, who cut me." I swallowed. "They wore sweatshirts with hoods. It made it harder to see them, even though they didn't have masks. I broke that one guy's nose. I heard him say it." More of their conversation came to mind. Their hands on me, pulling and tugging at my belt. A knee pressed into my thigh. "Look for tattooed men with records of sexual assault."

"Lex—"

"If he had more time, I don't know what would have happened. But the other one thought that was his plan. He told him not to."

Michael didn't react, but a newfound hatred burned in his eyes. "Do you remember anything else they said?"

I repeated every other tidbit I recalled.

"Do you think you would recognize their voices if you heard them again?"

"That's one thing I can't get out of my mind."

"We might be able to use that." He kissed me softly before moving toward the door. "Do you need anything? I want to make a few calls. I have some connections who might know something."

"I'm okay. Why don't you go back to the station and help them work the angles from there?"

"Because Amber won't be here for three more hours, and I'm not leaving you alone that long."

"You can. I'll be okay."

"If you were okay, you wouldn't have crawled back into bed as soon as you got home. The doctor said a week minimum. We can have this discussion again in a few days, but until then, you're stuck with a constant companion."

From the bedroom, I listened to Michael's deep voice. I couldn't quite make out the words, but I took comfort knowing he was close. Eventually, my eyelids drooped, and I stopped fighting my body's need to nap.

When I awoke, the throbbing in my head was back. Waking up was always the worst. It felt like I had a constant hangover without the fringe benefits of being happily intoxicated the night before. I blinked a few times, the pain dissipating.

"That concussion's taken a lot out of you," Michael whispered, and I turned to face him. "You slept through the night."

"What?" I looked at the clock. 8:02 a.m. "Shit."

"It's a good thing. The doctor said you need lots of rest. Amber said the extra sleep will speed up your recovery." Something was different about Michael. He seemed calmer, more at ease.

"Amber? When did you talk to her?"

"Last night. We had dinner, but we saved some for you. Would you rather have that instead of breakfast?"

I scrutinized his appearance. Reaching up, I pressed my fingers against a cut on his cheek. "How did this happen?"

"It's nothing." He took my hand in his, his knuckles bruised and swollen.

"Did you kill Kemper?"

"No." His eyes sparkled with mirth at my stupidity. At least I had a great excuse this time. I was suffering from a blow to the head. "On my way back from the station, I had a chat with a few informants." He looked away, unsure if he should admit anything else. "I had a hunch that I wanted to check out. Frank and I ended up making a few arrests. It probably won't lead to much, but Jack thinks one of the bozo wannabe Skulls we picked up might know something. We just have to convince him to talk."

The story wasn't making sense, but that might have had more to do with my impaired mental state than Michael's storytelling. Although, based on the condition of his knuckles, I had a feeling he was leaving out the violent details.

"You should ice your hand."

"Nah, it feels good. Cathartic. How are you feeling?"

"Better. I want to try to wean myself off the pain meds. Let's see what a few acetaminophen can do instead." I got out of bed, relieved the world felt stable. After wrapping my arm in plastic, I washed up and went into the kitchen so Michael could change my bandages.

After that was done, he heated the dinner I missed and watched me eat while he had coffee and eggs. When we were done, I settled onto the couch, unsure what to do with the rest of the day. Part of me wanted to go back to the station, but that would be against doctor's orders.

"Hey," he said, low and sexy, as he brushed my hair back. "You look like you're feeling a lot better today. I wanted to say I'm sorry about yesterday."

My fingers found their way into his hair, and we shared a real kiss for the first time in days.

He smiled. "I missed doing that. I hate it when we fight."

"Me too."

We kissed again, but he broke the kiss, backing

away. "Do you need anything else? I promised Jack I'd be in by nine."

"I'd like some dessert."

"I would too, but it's too soon. Doctor's orders." He winked. "The hospital would bring you green gelatin. How does that sound?"

"I hate gelatin."

"Well, if you promise to keep your hands to yourself, I'm sure I can find something better for you to eat."

"Is it just me or did that sound incredibly dirty?"

"Behave. We don't want your brain to turn into gelatin, and we both know that's precisely what happens every time I seduce you, even without a concussion."

"You wish."

"It is."

"Prove it."

"Not until you get medical clearance." He attempted a stern look, but his eyes gave it away. "I'll call Amber to chaperone if you plan on playing with fire."

"I don't want to play with fire. I want to play with you, but I'll behave. Scout's honor."

"Were you ever a girl scout?"

"Nope."

TWENTY-ONE

I flipped through the channels, but nothing held my attention. Amber had the day off, so Michael went back to work. The two men he and Frank arrested yesterday had records for B&E, assault, and possession of stolen property. They weren't to blame for the current spree, but Michael was positive they knew something about it. They weren't part of the Skulls' crew officially, but they ran in similar circles, with plenty of overlap. If the district attorney's office was willing to cut them a deal, Michael was sure he could persuade them to share insights on the Skulls' plan to decimate the police department's rank and file.

I hated what happened to Mr. Cline, me, and my colleagues. This needed to stop. More than anything, I wanted to nail these shitheads to the wall. But I was benched for the next few days.

Amber snatched the remote out of my hand and turned off the television. She gave me the stink eye and went back to the kitchen.

"What?" I asked.

"No TV. Flickering light patterns and fluctuations in volume aren't good for you." She finished making sandwiches, added carrot and celery sticks to the plates, and carried them over. "No caffeine either."

"Killjoy." I bit into a carrot stick. "Is ranch dressing banned too?"

"Don't even joke about such things." She went back to the kitchen and returned with the bottle.

I popped the top and gave it a sniff. It smelled okay, so I put a dollop on the side of my plate and dunked my carrot into it.

"Is that better?"

I chewed and swallowed. "Yep."

"Glad you think so."

"Okay, Amber, what's going on?" I put my plate on the coffee table.

"I don't like it."

"Well, you don't have to eat it."

"Not lunch. You getting hurt. I don't accept that as something that should ever happen. Those cops shouldn't be grilling you for answers. You're the one who's hurt. They should have to answer to you."

"I'll give you a hundred dollars if you march down to the station and tell Detective Lightman that."

"Lexie, I'm serious. Riley and I have spent way too much time together on account of you being asleep seventy-five percent of the time. He said you weren't happy with the job before this happened. You want a promotion, but is that really the answer?"

"He thinks it is."

"That doesn't mean he's right. Do you even want to be a detective? You never mentioned it to me until recently, until all that shit went down when you were working vice."

"You know I never wanted to work vice."

"Yeah, but I thought you wanted to help people, do some kind of outreach thing, community policing or whatever."

"That's not a separate thing. I never wanted to be

Officer Friendly."

"Who?"

"I want to help people, Amber. I want to make sure they're safe. That's all I've ever wanted. Patrol officers show up first. They're on the front lines, but they can only do so much. Investigations are how we stop the bigger fish, the ones who are sending out the little fish to break people's kneecaps and bash in their skulls."

"Why do I get the feeling you aren't talking euphemistically?"

"I'm not."

"You could do something else, Lexie. Go into social work."

"That's not really my thing."

"Why do you want to be around the danger? Is it because that's what you're used to?"

"Don't be ridiculous."

"Your extended family has done a lot of questionable things. You've always been on the periphery of violence. It's why your parents didn't want you to become a cop in the first place."

"That's because they were afraid I'd have to arrest our relatives."

"That's entirely my point." She sighed. "Have you called them to tell them what happened? I bet your uncle could find out who attacked you."

"I don't want to do things that way."

"Regardless, your parents would want to know. Do they even know you're dating a detective?"

"No, and that's irrelevant." I took an angry bite of my sandwich and swallowed. "How do you think they'd react to me being hurt on the job?"

"They'd tell you exactly what I'm going to tell you." Amber swallowed the lump in her throat and looked me straight in the eye. "Walk away. You don't need this shit." She ran a hand through her hair. "I'm getting pre-mature grays because of you."

"That's because you're an old maid."

"Shut up. You're only five months younger than me. And old maids do not have sex with a paramedic in the back of his rig, so go fish."

"Go fish?"

"I don't know. You're making me crazy."

I narrowed my eyes. "You had sex in the back of an ambulance?"

"Yeah, so?"

"You're a hospital administrator."

She gave me a confused look. "Do you think I should have reserved one of the on-call rooms instead? This isn't a soapy primetime TV show."

Shaking it off, I decided I didn't even want to know. "Amber, despite everything, and we both know there's been a lot of everything, I think I could love this job if the circumstances are right."

"And if you don't get promoted to detective, then what?"

"I don't know."

"You need a plan B."

"Michael and I take precautions. We don't need Plan B."

She glared at me. "That's not what I meant, and you know it. But I'm glad you're safe."

"Yep." I thought about Lightman's words from the night before. "When do you think I can go back to work? Nothing rigorous, just light duty, sitting behind a desk, that type of thing."

"After the doctor gives you the go-ahead, and," she emphasized the word, "you can stay awake an entire day without popping any type of pain reliever, even the OTC ones."

"Okay." At least now I had a goal to work toward. I'd get there, sooner rather than later. "Any idea how long until Michael and I can get reacquainted?"

"Oh my god, you are such a prude. You can't say fuck like rabbits?"

I smirked. "Fuck like rabbits."

"I don't know. Ask the doctor. Do I look like some sort of medical professional?"

"A little bit, if the light catches you just right."

"You should have your eyes checked." She grinned. "Little Lexie Sarconi is all grown up and wants to date a boy."

"Shut up." I laughed, throwing a pillow at her.

"Seriously, I'd say you should wait for the bruising to go away. If not, I don't think it'll be a very pleasant experience for you." She raised an eyebrow. "Was he hoping to get some? Because if he's pressuring you, I'd be more than happy to—"

"No, Mother," I said, "he's not pressuring me. I may have been pressuring him."

"Damn, now I know we've been friends too long. All my naughty girl tendencies have rubbed off on you. Whatever happened to your 'no sex unless we're in a committed, loving relationship' philosophy?"

"We are in a committed, loving relationship. If I remember correctly, you helped make that happen."

"I also remember you being pissed off that I stuck my nose where it didn't belong. I was right then, and I'm right now." Amber gave me a look. "But that's not why you jumped Riley's bones the first time. That was because you turned into a naughty girl."

"No. It's because I freaked out that my new boyfriend could be killed on the job."

"And now you're freaking out because you were almost killed, and in order to forget about that, you want to get some. I'd suggest you take a cold shower and don't dwell, unless the end result is finding another job that is less dangerous."

I glared at her and took our empty lunch plates to the sink. After washing and drying them, I spent the rest of the day in the living room studying for the detective's exam. Thirteen days to go. But the questions and scenarios kept reminding me of the ongoing case against the Skulls. I wasn't sure if any of the material was getting absorbed, but I couldn't really worry about that now.

When my head started to hurt and my eyes burned, I put my notes down. My apartment looked like a flower shop. I had eight different floral arrangements, ranging from a single flower to an entire bouquet of yellow roses, an upgrade Kemper had sent as a follow-up apology after the incident with Michael. In addition to that, the gangs unit sent over a fruit basket, probably a bribe to get me back to work that much sooner.

"Maybe you should try to rest," Amber suggested.

"I don't think sitting on the couch and reading counts as exercise."

"It's exercise for your brain. And I know you're just being stubborn to prove a point." She gave me that annoying know-it-all look of hers. "I said you can't go back to work or boff your boyfriend's brains out until you spend an entire day up and awake without pain meds." She held out the bottle of acetaminophen. "Today is not that day."

"I'm fine."

"I love you like a sister. You're my best friend and my partner in crime. I'd do absolutely anything for you, so even if you don't want to hear it, someone has to say it. And Michael is too much of a pussy to stand up to you. But you don't need to do this."

"Clearly, you don't know him very well. He's supporting me. He isn't intimidated by a strong woman, like my shit-for-brains ex. He wants me to succeed. Why don't you?"

"It's not that. And I'll give your boyfriend some credit. He's smart enough to pick his battles. But he's been brainwashed into thinking being a cop is an excellent idea. It isn't. You told me to always be honest with you, so there it is. I won't bring it up again."

"Good, because I don't want to hear it. And when I told you to be honest with me, I meant whether an outfit makes me look fat or if bangs are a bad idea."

"Bangs are always a bad idea, and something that makes you look fat, puh-lease." She glanced at the bandage on my arm. "Have you seen it yet?"

I nodded. "It doesn't change anything."

"I spoke to the head of plastics at the hospital. He said they may be able to laser it to even the scar, kind of how they get rid of tattoos. It'll depend on how much it's raised. If that's not an option, he mentioned skin grafts would be a possibility."

"That sounds extreme."

"It's an option. You don't have to take it. You can do whatever you want. In the meantime, he said he'd personally perform the follow-up once things have healed. There are some really good creams and new treatments that might be able to minimize the appearance without surgical intervention."

"Thanks for asking."

"Of course." She hugged me. "Once the stitches are out, I bet it won't be so bad."

"Am, why didn't you follow through with the whole nursing thing instead of switching to administration?"

"The pay was better and no icky bodily fluids."

"But you loved all those science classes."

"No bodily fluids in science class." She moved in closer. "I don't know if you've figured this out yet, but people are gross. The human body can be absolutely disgusting. And administration comes with better job security."

"Bullshit."

"And hot paramedic ass."

"That's slightly more believable." I crossed my arms, waiting for her to admit the truth.

"And because I wanted to help and couldn't stomach being on the front lines as a nurse." She sighed. "Fine, maybe I get the whole detective thing. But it's just us against the world, so you can't let the world kick your ass again. I can't save us by myself. And Detective Stud can't replace you. He looks like he'd refuse to spend the entire day bargain-hunting for designer shoes, so I need my Lexie to stay in one piece."

"Michael might not bargain-hunt, but he will spend an evening at the art gallery. And he uses the fancy salon conditioner, but don't tell him I told you that."

"No way." She gaped. "I didn't peg him for that," her eyes darted back and forth, "but come to think of it, his hair does do that perfect bounce but stay in place thing. And he is ripped. What does he look like when he plays dress-up?"

"You've seen him in his work clothes." Michael almost always wore a button-up shirt with a suit jacket to conceal his gun and handcuffs when he wasn't working the streets.

"No, I mean taking you to some fancy restaurant dressed up."

"A little like an international spy, but he has all the James Bonds beat."

Amber studied me for a long moment. "I've just decided what we're going to do to celebrate once you're fully recovered."

"Does it involve stealing Michael's conditioner?"

"No, well, maybe. But I say we go on a double date

someplace that requires reservations and has a dress code."

TWENTY-TWO

When Michael came home that evening, Amber graciously bowed out, saying she had dinner plans and she'd be back tomorrow after work to check on me. Michael entered the bedroom, expecting me to be asleep. I waved to him, and he laughed.

"She's in a good mood. Did you have fun today?" he asked.

"A little, in between studying and begging to watch TV. Oh, and she also tricked me into agreeing to a double date with her and a hot paramedic. Sorry about that."

He scrunched his brows together. "Jay?"

"Who's Jay?"

"The EMT who comforted her at the hospital." He laid his gun and cuffs on the nightstand. "I didn't know they were together." He went to the closet to hang up his suit jacket. "It makes sense, but she never mentioned it."

"Why would she mention it to you?"

"To make conversation." He rubbed his eyes. "We ran out of things to talk about. There are only so many 'did Lexie ever tell you about the time' stories to share." He crinkled his nose playfully. "How are you feeling?"

"I was feeling better before you told me you and my best friend were exchanging blackmail worthy stories about me." I climbed out of bed and wrapped my arms around him. "Did you convince them to cooperate? Have any other arrests been made?"

"No, but we'll get them. It's just a matter of time."

"I need to get back to work."

Michael smiled. "You're getting antsy." He put an arm around my shoulders and led the way into the kitchen. "How about I make dinner? I'll even let you watch as I perform my best cooking show host impression." He saw the question in my eyes. "And I'll tell you what's happening with the case because I know that's what you want."

~*~

"Well?" Michael grinned from ear to ear.

"It was delicious. But your delivery could use some work, and you definitely lose points on plating. Overall, I'd give you a seven."

"You know I'm more than a seven." He gave me a sexy look.

"Fine. You're an eight."

He cleared his throat.

"Does that extra half inch really mean so much to you?"

He made a tsk sound. "I thought you promised to keep your mind out of the gutter. Inches are not how chefs are ranked. It's a point system. Why in the world would you go there?"

I threw the balled-up dish towel at him. "You went there."

"I'd like to go there." He gave me a wicked smile. "Culinary school, that is."

"That's what you're calling it now?"

"Well, it has the same first two letters, and if we move the n in front of the l, then—"

"Michael," I shrieked, laughing. My cheeks on fire.

"They both involve savoring a mouth-watering experience."

I exhaled, getting up to clear the table. "You're killing me."

He swooped in and took the plates from my hands, nuzzling against my neck before continuing to the sink. After rinsing the dishes and putting them in the dishwasher, he went into the living room and returned to the kitchen table with a stack of folders.

"Are you sure you want to do this?" he asked.

"There's not much else I can do." Since Michael brought work home, I knew the police department needed my help. "Don't worry. I'm feeling okay."

"All right, but if your head starts to hurt or you get tired, promise you'll say something. I don't want this to make you worse. You know exactly what the incentive is for getting better."

"I get to help Detective Lightman on the case?" I asked innocently.

"The other incentive."

I played dumb. "Going out with Amber and her new beau on a double date?"

"No dessert for you. Ever."

"I bet part of you would disagree." I glanced down at his crotch. "What did we say? You're a seven?"

He licked his lips, shaking his head, and laughing. "Damn, you're feisty." He wrapped his arms around my shoulders and kissed my neck. "I'm so glad you're feeling better, sweetheart." He brushed his lips against my earlobe before letting me go. "You've had me worried for days."

"I'm sorry. I never wanted to make you worry. We just need to make sure these assholes don't do it to someone else."

For the next two hours, we read reports. Mostly, Michael read them to me while I looked at the pictures. "There's one other thing. Are you feeling up to it? You can say no."

"I'm fine. Really. What is it?"

Michael went to the coat closet and took a recorder out of his pocket. "I made a copy of the 9-1-1 call, the anonymous tip about the liquor store being ransacked. The call came from a prepaid phone. Whoever made it went to a lot of trouble to conceal his identity. A court order was issued to trace the number back to the credit card, which was also prepaid. But Jack thinks we can trace it back to where it was purchased and get the caller's identity that way."

"Hit play," I said. "I want to hear it."

He put the recorder on the table between us. As soon as the caller spoke, my blood ran cold. It was the man who carved that message into my arm. I picked up the device and hit stop. I'd heard enough.

"That's him. That's the asshole who did this." I held up my arm, so angry I was practically shaking. "There's no doubt about it. Once we ID him, I'll testify to it."

"Let me call Jack and tell him." Michael reached for his phone, giving me an uncertain look. "Are you okay?"

"I swear to god if you ask me that again, I'm going to scream. Nothing about this is okay. But I don't want you to coddle me. I want these bastards locked away."

"I want them in a fucking hole." He inhaled. "But don't expect me not to ask if you're okay. Because I'm not. And I know you can't be. But asking is the only thing I can do."

I grabbed his free hand as he put the phone to his

ear. "Okay."

He gave me a small smile. "Okay."

I picked up a pen and grabbed the legal pad Michael had been using for notes. While he updated Lightman on the situation, I wrote down my theories on the dynamics of the trio. When Michael hung up, he tried to read over my shoulder.

"Two men do the heavy lifting. An alpha and a beta. The one who called in the tip is the alpha. He set us up. He wanted to inflict maximum damage, and he wanted to do it slowly."

"He's probably a sadist."

"And a predator," I said.

"Almost all of them are." Michael watched as I sketched out a pyramid shape. "What about the other two?"

"They didn't have much of a say. It wasn't a democracy, but the other one, not the one who shot Kemper and fled, but the second one, he seemed the most rational. He wanted things to go smoothly. In and out. No wasting time. No getting caught."

"But you don't think he was in charge?"

"No."

"What about the third guy? The one who shot Kemper?"

"He darted past us. At first, I thought he panicked. But I think it was a ploy. If Kemper hadn't gone after him, he may have turned at the door and shot one of us in the head. Either way, the third unsub was the distraction."

"He wanted to separate the two of you."

"I can't be sure. It all went down so fast. It was one thing after another. The three unsubs would disappear in the dark. It was hard to keep them straight. They all had such similar builds, particularly in the shadows." I thought about it, but I had no way of knowing what the third man's plan had been. "Maybe I should have tried to help Kemper."

"You couldn't have. You were dealing with two offenders. You had to make sure they were secure before assisting. That's basic. If anything, Kemper should have let the third unsub go."

"Except we have no way of knowing what would have happened if he did. Like I said, that could have been what they were hoping for. The end result could have been worse."

"Now you're speculating," Michael said.

"Why did they pick that liquor store?" I asked. "They lured us there on purpose. But why there?"

"At that time of night, no one's around. It's pretty desolate. The cameras were easy to take out. And there aren't a lot of street cams nearby."

"Do you think they knocked over the place before?"

"We looked. No break-ins or robberies have been reported in the last three years."

I tried to think. "Assuming they hit the convenience store first, there are only so many routes they could have taken to get to the liquor store. They must have been seen leaving or arriving."

"There was enough time in between for them to have gone from point a to point c before returning to point b, but Sam is reviewing traffic cam footage from that neighborhood. She's hoping we'll spot them somewhere along the way."

"How did they get away? Did they have a car waiting? The clerk at the convenience store never said."

"If they had a getaway vehicle, we haven't found it. But if it's there, Sam will spot it." Michael made a note to follow up.

Leaning back in the chair, I rubbed my eyes, hoping he wouldn't realize my headache had returned. "The prepaid credit card might be our best bet, but that seems like a crapshoot."

"We'll figure it out. We have his voice on tape. That led to all this." Michael gestured at the pages of notes. "It's just a matter of time."

"What about the latest jewelry store robbery? Preston and Lightman said another place was hit, and the owner feared for his life. Did anything happen with that? The thieves didn't come back and finish him off, did they?" The panic crept into my voice, despite my best efforts to play it cool.

"Nothing's happened yet. Everyone's fine. But the owner won't help us. He denies a crime ever took place, despite the smashed display cases and missing merchandise. Without a report, there is no crime. Assuming the Skulls were hoping that newest break-in would put us in their crosshairs, they'll have to try something else to force our hand."

"That's what I'm afraid of." I reached for the file, but Michael put his hand over mine.

"That's enough for tonight, Lexie."

TWENTY-THREE

I didn't sleep well. Every time I drifted off, I was back in the liquor store. I shot straight up in bed, gasping.

"Lexie, what's wrong?" Michael asked. He scanned the room, his hand moving toward his gun.

"Nightmares. It's nothing. Go back to sleep."

"Fuck." He turned on the light and brushed a damp strand of hair away from my face.

"I'm okay. Knowing progress is being made and working on the case makes me feel better, even if it means a few bad dreams." I snorted. "At least I'm dreaming again. I almost forgot what sleep was like without high-powered pain meds."

"Shall I get you a painkiller?" he asked, watching as I rubbed my forehead and shifted against the pillows to get comfortable.

"No. It'll go away. Whenever I wake up, my head always hurts. Can you turn off the light, though? That's not helping."

He reached over and flipped the switch. My breath hitched involuntarily, and he sat up.

"You're not okay. Come here, honey." He maneuvered around until I was able to lean against his chest with my head propped on his shoulder. He wrapped his arms around my waist, asking, "Is this okay? Does it hurt?"

"Not at all. You worry too much." I turned my face into his neck and inhaled. "I hate being so weak. I should be tougher."

"You're the strongest woman I know. Nightmares and getting hurt don't make you weak, Lexie. It's what you do afterward that defines your strength. You refuse to let them win. Even now, you won't back down. That's real strength."

"Or stupidity," I said, thinking of Amber's insistence that I walk away. "I just want things to go back to normal."

"They will. Give it time."

"I hate waiting."

He smiled through the darkness and kissed me. I returned the kiss, and a contented sigh escaped from his throat when we broke for air.

"No sex," he whispered.

"No sex," I agreed, letting my fingers trace his defined jaw before my mouth latched onto his soft, supple lips and my hands were lost in his hair.

Michel Riley had many talents. One of which was being an excellent kisser. Most of our kisses were slow, lengthy exchanges. His lips firmly brushed against mine, first in short little teases before pressing more urgently and breaking away with a resounding pop.

I wanted to be lost in his lips for the rest of the night. He leaned in, so close we shared oxygen, our mouths open, dancing together. The process repeated until we were breathless, seconds away from doing more than kissing.

Michael's phone buzzed. I stared at it, watching the light emanate from beneath. Something else happened. They wouldn't be calling otherwise.

Michael ran his fingers through my hair before

sitting up and grabbing the phone. "Go for Riley."

I licked my lips which already felt chapped and dropped my head against the pillow, watching Michael's chest rise and fall. I could practically hear his heart hammering a frenzied rhythm.

"When?" he asked. Every muscle in his body went rigid. "I'm on my way."

"What happened?" I asked as soon as he put the phone down.

"We received a tip about a gunshot victim at an animal hospital. When patrol arrived on the scene, they found a few bloody bandages and some trophies the assholes took off their previous victims."

"Trophies?" I remembered my missing gun and badge. "What kind of trophies?"

Michael ignored my question and got out of bed, digging through his overnight bag for a change of clothes. "It doesn't matter. One of them was hiding in a storage closet with a shotgun."

My stomach jumped into my throat. "How bad?"

"Bad."

"Who was it?"

"Jacob Evans."

I'd ridden with Evans once or twice. He was a quiet guy. The only thing he talked about was his fiancé and all the kids they wanted to have. "Did we get the shooter?"

Michael shook his head. "They split up during the search. It was the storage closet nearest the exit. The unsub fired once, dumped the gun, and ran. By the time anyone made it to Evans, the unsub had already gotten away. The only good thing about this is we have security footage."

I got out of bed and went to my dresser. "I'm coming with you."

"Lexie, you aren't cleared."

"I don't care. Lightman said I can work a desk. Right now, there's a lot going on. The least I can do is help sort through it all. We can't let them get away again. I can't stay here and do nothing. I need to be there."

"All right, but if you need to take a break or go home, you better do it." Michael stared at me. "I mean it, Lex."

"Yes, sir."

When we arrived at the crime scene, I followed Michael. Lightman was standing in the doorway, staring down at the floor, his hand over his mouth. Detective Frank Devereaux was studying the exam table and the layout.

"Sarconi heard what happened," Michael said. "She wants to help."

Lightman turned, eyeing me up and down. I wasn't in uniform. I didn't even have my service piece or badge. Instead, I had my backup and a spare set of cuffs shoved in my purse. Medical hadn't cleared me, but it was the middle of the night. Lightman had to know that.

"How'd you hear about this?" Lightman asked me.

"I told her," Michael said before I could respond.

Lightman scrutinized me. "You might as well see what we found." He gestured toward the storage closet. The crime scene markers and blood spatter on the floor indicated this was where Evans had been shot. On the shelf inside the closet were two police badges. One of them was mine.

"I didn't know he took that," I said. "They have my gun too, don't they?"

"We recovered your weapon. It's been in evidence, awaiting your medical clearance. You should have said something about the badge."

Things had been such a blur, I hadn't even thought

about it. Michael hadn't mentioned it. Neither had Preston or the LT. "No one told me."

Lightman didn't want to hear any excuses. In fact, I wasn't even sure he cared that I had failed to report my badge being stolen. But that was something the review board would frown on. Why hadn't anyone said anything to me?

"They left your badge and Kemper's here on purpose. They wanted us to know it was them. They set us up, just like they set you and Kemper up at the liquor store," Lightman said.

"The anonymous tip."

Lightman jerked his head in Detective Devereaux's direction. "Frank will catch you up, Mike. I'm heading back to the office to get the ball-rolling on search warrants and subpoenas. I'll take Sarconi with me. I want her to listen to the latest 9-1-1 call."

Michael nodded, barely looking in my direction, before crossing the room to join Detective Devereaux.

"Sir, I didn't—" I began once I was seated in the passenger's seat of Lightman's cruiser.

"Save it, Sarconi. I don't want an apology. You had more important things to worry about than what those assholes did with your badge. I'd never fault you for that."

"You reported it for me," I said, realizing Lightman had covered my ass even if my own report failed to mention it.

He glanced at me. "Gangs protects its own."

Whether I wanted to work for the unit or not, Lightman had decided I was part of the team. I wasn't sure if Preston had set that in motion or if Michael had pled my case for me. But none of it mattered now. That was tomorrow's problem. "How's Evans?"

"He's in surgery. We're hoping he'll pull through."

I bit my lip and stared out the window. "This has to

stop."

"No shit."

Once we arrived, Lightman stuck me at an empty desk near the rear of the bullpen. "As far as I'm concerned, you're not here. But come morning, I need you to get cleared for desk duty, and then I'm going to need your ass back in this chair."

"I'll do my best."

"Do better than that." He dropped a stack of files in front of me. "I don't have time to catch you up. I'm assuming that's already been taken care of, but if not, familiarize yourself. I'll get a copy of that recording for you to listen to. If you tell me it's the same guy who attacked you, the same guy who lured you into a trap at the liquor store, then we'll take it from there."

"Yes, sir."

TWENTY-FOUR

Talk about hitting the ground running. The gangs unit had so many things in the works I wasn't sure where to start. My head was spinning, and I didn't think it was from the concussion.

Lightman had me listen to the anonymous tip which had been phoned in regarding the man with the gunshot wound. The same voice I heard in my nightmares played from the speaker.

"That's him," I said.

Lightman didn't ask if I was sure. "It was another trap. Based on what we found in the vet's office, he waited until his buddy was patched up before he decided to alert us." He plugged a USB into the side of the computer. "The surveillance footage shows three of them inside. They wanted us to see this. They're getting more brazen."

"They wore masks," I said.

"I said brazen, not stupid." Lightman bit his upper lip, reminding me of a pug with an underbite. "Watch this. Maybe it'll ring a bell. I've got calls to make."

"Yes, sir."

I settled in. The last thing I wanted to see was Officer Evans get shot. No one had shown me the infrared feed from when Kemper and I were attacked, but everyone who spoke about it made it sound gruesome. And that only involved heat signatures. I didn't know what this would entail.

The first thing I noticed was the men weren't wearing gas masks, which is what the thieves involved in the tagging and the break-ins had worn. Instead, they wore surgical masks, as if making a mockery of whatever patch job they performed on their injured comrade.

Grabbing a legal pad, I made two columns and wrote down the obvious differences. Pausing the footage, I examined the three men. Their identities remained hidden, concealed beneath the masks and their hooded jackets. They wore gloves. Maybe we could get shoeprints. I made a note and continued watching the footage.

One of them had a broken nose, but I couldn't figure out which one. The one I'd shot appeared to have been grazed. The security cameras didn't pick up the amateur surgery they performed, but based on the way the third guy moved, he must have gotten hit near his back ribs. He moved okay for a guy with a week-old bullet wound, but he favored his left side and remained slightly hunched.

"Detective Lightman," I asked when he returned from making his phone calls, "was anything taken from the vet's office?"

"Like what?"

"Antibiotics or painkillers."

"We'll find out in a few hours when we finish clearing the scene." He read my notes. "You don't think the tip about the GSW was just a ploy?"

"Not with all those bloody bandages and surgical tools you found." A thought came to mind. "What about DNA?"

"Even if we put a rush on it, we're looking at weeks

before we get results or a match."

"They were so careful with other things. Why wouldn't they be more careful with DNA evidence?"

Lightman shrugged. "Maybe they didn't think about it, or they don't think their DNA is in our system."

"Is that possible?"

"Compelling DNA isn't as easy as fingerprints."

"Did Detective Riley mention I think this guy," I pointed to the paused screen where the man I believed to be the ringleader had just taken something from his pocket and placed it on the shelf before stepping into the large storage closet, "may have a record for sexual assault?"

"Which would mean we'd have his DNA on file." Lightman thought about it. "You have no proof, but you're a cop who spent a lot of time around the type. I'll defer to your assessment on that. However, that doesn't mean the bastard was ever caught. It's also possible his accomplices don't share the same taste when it comes to committing crimes."

I unpaused the footage, watching as he closed himself inside the closet. His accomplices had left minutes earlier. Now it was just him and the cops. "Do you think they want no part of this? Killing cops is a dangerous crime to commit."

"They should have thought about that sooner." Lightman stared at the screen, watching as two patrol officers entered. They went past the storage closet, heading for the bright lights in the exam room. Another two patrol officers entered. The four reconvened near the front door, feet away from the waiting unsub. They split up, hoping to search every inch of the place. Before Evans could open the closet door, Lightman paused the feed. "I've seen it once. I don't need to watch it again." He flicked my notes.

"You're sure we're looking at two different teams?"

"It's the only thing that makes sense, unless they have multiple personalities. But they tried to kill Kemper and me. They nearly succeeded. But the attack that happened after ours, the one on Sanchez and Hawking, that was tame in comparison."

"Until the attack tonight, which almost took off Evans' head." Lightman pointed to the screen. "These assholes are piggybacking off the thieves, unless they are working in tandem. See what you can find out." He pulled a sheet of paper from one of the folders and put it on top. "That's every relevant case number. Separate them out and look for patterns."

"Didn't you already do this?" I asked, recalling Michael and I theorizing on this exact thing not that long ago.

"Do it again." And with that, Lightman disappeared down the hallway.

I spent the rest of the night doing as he asked. It wasn't necessarily new, but there was a lot more of it than I realized. The Skulls declaration of war meant every tagged location and break-in had to be assessed. With the sheer volume of calls, I wondered if word had spread and other thieves and gangs hoped to pass the blame for the crimes they were committing on to the Skulls.

Once morning came, I excused myself and went to get that medical clearance. After lots of cajoling and a bit of begging, I convinced the doctor to sign the paperwork. He stipulated limited desk duty. That was it. But it was enough to make Lightman happy and to put me on the right side of things, should a review board have questions.

When I returned, I gave Lt. Peterson a copy of the paperwork and went back to work in the gangs' bullpen.

"Hey, Lexie. How are you feeling?" Detective Preston asked, tucking her bag into her bottom desk drawer.

"I would say better, but after hearing what happened last night, I don't know."

"Evans is out of surgery. He's still critical, but the odds are in his favor." She looked around, finding everyone else was too hard at work to linger at their desks. "Have you seen Michael around?"

"No. Why?"

She hesitated. "I'm afraid he's planning to do something stupid, and someone needs to talk him out of it."

"What happened?"

"Nothing yet." She got up and joined me at my desk. "When he and Frank returned from the crime scene, they went straight into the interrogation rooms. Did Michael tell you they made a couple of arrests two nights ago?"

"I didn't think that panned out yet."

"It's getting there. He and Frank have been encouraging the suspects to be more compliant."

I didn't like the way she said it, especially when I thought about the cut on Michael's cheek and his swollen knuckles. "Interrogations are recorded, and Frank was in there with him. What's the problem?"

"No problem." She rested her hips against my desk and leaned down. "Mike got them to give up a black market jeweler. That man's name is Ralph Kazinski. Kazinski gets his supply of gems and gold from somewhere, and we've posited the thieves who knocked over Mr. Cline's jewelry store are his source."

"Shouldn't someone follow up?"

"Jack's on his way to pay Kazinski a visit, but if the thieves aren't behind the violent and vicious attacks on the police, then we still have nothing. Michael is fit to be tied. I'm afraid what he might do."

"He won't do anything. He knows better."

She gave me a sad look. "I hope you're right."

TWENTY-FIVE

I hadn't moved from the desk in hours. But I hadn't come up with anything brilliant either. My gut knew we were looking at two different groups of offenders. Besides making calls and doing whatever menial tasks the detectives needed, all I did was go through mugshots. Instead of focusing on the tattoos, like I previously had done, I was looking for men who fit my vague recollection. Particularly, I was hoping to find the asshole who shot Officer Evans and carved a message into my arm, if for no other reason than I wanted to deliver a message of my own. The stitched-up flesh might say "You're Mine," but this bastard was definitely going to be mine.

"Breathe," I reminded myself, feeling my blood pressure spike which made my ever-present headache worse. Rubbing my eyes, I looked around. Lightman had brought Kazinski in hours ago. Detective Devereaux was at his desk, making calls and watching video footage. I had no idea where Preston and Riley had gone.

Getting up, I was reminded of the dull ache in my torso, which radiated through my sides to my back. I grunted a little as I made my way toward the break room to get another cup of coffee. Amber most certainly would not approve. Neither would my doctor.

"Hey, Lexie," Devereaux looked up as I moved past him, "the couch in there is pretty comfortable. Why don't you make use of it?"

"I'm okay."

"Maybe do it anyway, at least until someone else gets back. I'm not great in emergency situations. I don't want to have to call the paramedics if you pass out."

"You're a cop, Frank. How can you not be good in emergency situations?"

"That's a different kind of emergency." He winked. "Humor me. We already have enough of our own in the hospital. I don't want you to have to go back."

"Do you want a refill?" I picked up his coffee cup.

"I can get it."

"I'll do it. You're working on something important."

"I take it you can't make an ID."

"Not a visual one. I thought something would jog my memory, but all the faces are blurring together. I don't think I ever got a good enough look at him." I took Devereaux's cup, refilled it, and returned it to his desk. But I didn't get a cup for myself. Instead, I went back into the break room, found a bottle of acetaminophen in the cabinet, took two with a hefty sip of water and stretched out on the couch. Detective Devereaux was right. It was pretty comfy.

With my eyes closed, I ran through every detail again. Maybe we could trace the guns. The unsub left the shotgun he used to shoot Evans at the latest scene. We had the bullet from the alleyway. It had been compromised by the brick wall, but ballistics may still be able to determine something useful. But either way, we had the shotgun. It had to lead us somewhere.

After twenty minutes of resting with my eyes

closed, which turned into forty-five, I returned to the bullpen. Devereaux's back was to me. He put down the phone, bowed his head, and let out an audible exhale. I wasn't sure if that was good or bad, and I was a little afraid to find out.

"Is everything okay?" I asked.

"That was the hospital. Evans is awake."

"Oh, thank god." I made the same sound Devereaux had.

"He's not out of the woods yet, but it's something. Mike's hoping to get a chance to talk to him. We need to put this thing to bed."

"Damn straight," Lightman said, entering the bullpen. "I just heard. Anything else I should know?"

"They had two getaway vehicles. The injured unsub was assisted into a black sedan by his pal. The car had no plates, and we never get a clear view of the VIN. It looks like they parked it in this garage." Devereaux indicated the square on an aerial map. "Patrol is searching for it now, but this isn't much to go on. And they have yet to find a single vehicle missing a plate."

"They must have put them back on. What about footage from the cameras inside the garage?"

"We have to wait for the judge to get back from lunch before we can get him to sign the court order."

"This is fucking ridiculous." Lightman put his hands on his hips. "This is why our justice system moves so damn slowly." Shaking it off, he turned to me. "Do you have anything for me?"

"Not really. I was just about to see if ballistics had anything on the shotgun or the bullet they pulled from the alleyway where Kemper and I were originally ambushed."

"You think those were the same guys?"

"I don't know, sir."

Lightman considered my words. "Some shithead

who hides in a closet to try to blow off a man's head wouldn't have fired a warning shot."

"He wouldn't," I said, "but his accomplices might."

"Interesting." Lightman headed for the double doors without another word.

"Is he always like that?" I asked.

"You don't remember?" Devereaux chuckled. "That's Jack, especially when he's stressed. He's been going at Kazinski nonstop for the last six hours. Kazinski's attorney has threatened to file charges against us, and the brass is getting concerned."

"That's bullshit. Kazinski's our best bet at identifying the thieves, unless the traffic cams or prepaid credit card lead somewhere solid." I'd almost forgotten about that until the words left my mouth. "Did you get anything on that yet?"

"It'll take time. We can track down where the card was purchased based on where it was activated. Unfortunately, the credit card company said it could take up to three days to get the information."

"So you are up to speed," Preston said, joining us. "I'm surprised Michael told you about all that. Did he also tell you what he wants to do?"

"We haven't spoken today." I hadn't even glimpsed Michael since returning to the station.

Devereaux sighed. "What dumbass thing does he want to do now?"

"He thinks we should cut Kazinski loose, put a tail on him, and hope he leads us to our killer thieves."

"That won't work if we're looking at two separate groups," I said.

"It will if they're connected." Preston studied the images on Devereaux's computer screen.

"Do we have any basis for thinking that?" Devereaux asked.

"Besides the obvious, that this is far too

coincidental?" She shook her head. "No. We have no basis for thinking anything."

"Maybe we should try Riley's plan," I said, figuring I should have Michael's back.

"You don't understand. Lieutenant Peterson won't let us cut Kazinski loose because it'll give credence to his complaints that he's been mistreated. It'll make us look like we're wrong, even though we aren't."

"We have to do something," Devereaux said. "I'm sure if Jack agrees, he'll get us authorization."

"Let's hope he does it before Michael does something stupid."

"Like what?" I asked.

"I told him he needs to get his head screwed on straight. Last night must have knocked the damn screws loose again," Devereaux said. "I'll have a talk with him."

"I don't think it'll help. Michael's prepared to take one for the team. He'll say he fed his CIs the intel on Kazinski so we could bring him in. Under those circumstances, the DA will drop the charges and let Kazinski go, regardless of what the brass says."

"Mike won't do that," Devereaux said. "He's just venting. Ignore the crazy talk, Sam. You know he's all bark."

She looked at me before looking away. "This time's different."

"You always think that. But Mikey's a good cop. Shit like that would end his career. He'd never do anything like that. He just gets pissed and runs his mouth. We all do. That's the beginning and end of it."

More than anything, I hoped Devereaux was right.

"Where is he?" I asked.

"Outside interrogation," Preston said.

Nodding, I excused myself. Under normal conditions, I wouldn't second-guess a detective. But nothing about this situation was normal.

I went through the double doors, pausing when I heard Lt. Peterson say, "The department received another threat. This time, the message was spray-painted on the side of a patrol car, which had responded to a report of another robbery."

"What did it say?" Michael asked.

"Stay out of our way."

"At least they were to the point." Michael put his hands on his hips. "Was anyone hurt this time?"

"No. The taggers painted the car and took off before the officers returned. It couldn't have been more than a couple of minutes. Several witnesses saw it happen. One even recorded it on his phone and posted the video online."

"Dial it up." Michael peered over the lieutenant's shoulder, watching the footage on the tablet. "Right there. Aren't those the men Sarconi and Kemper stopped outside the sex shop? The ones who filed a complaint?"

Peterson zoomed in. "It looks like it. Ask Sarconi to take a look."

When Michael turned to get me, he was surprised to find me standing behind him. "I guess you heard."

"Let me see." I took the tablet from his hand. "Those are the same men. I hope now we can bring them in."

Peterson smiled at me. "Absolutely. I would say you could do the honors, but that wouldn't be good for anyone. I'll send a unit to collect them."

"Given everything that's been going on, you might want to send SWAT," Michael said.

"Yeah, we'll see. Good catch." Peterson returned to his office and picked up his phone.

I stared at the spot where the tablet had been.

"Hey." Michael lowered his voice, but he didn't step

closer. With so many officers nearby, it was best if he kept a respectable distance. "What are you doing out here? Are you looking for someone to take you home?"

Before he could call an officer over, I said, "Preston thinks you're going to do something stupid. Devereaux said you wouldn't, but I wanted to make sure."

"It's not stupid, Lexie. I have a good plan. Jack's considering it, but he thinks we should wait. The problem is, the longer we wait, the worse things could get. What if they target you again?"

The blood drained from my face. "Why would they?"

"They left your badge in that closet and carved that message into your arm for a reason." He looked down at where I was cradling my forearm in my other hand, absently rubbing against the tape at the end of the bandage. "This is far from over. The more of them we bring in, the more likely they are to retaliate. We need answers, and waiting for something to shake loose isn't working. Officer Evans nearly died."

"He'll be okay."

"Half his face is missing. How is that okay?" Michael looked around, realizing he'd raised his voice and garnered the attention of several nearby officers. "They keep setting traps for us. I say it's time we set a trap for them."

I turned and headed for the gangs unit. Michael followed. As soon as I came across an empty conference room, I went inside. He entered behind me and shut the door. We left the lights off, so hopefully, no one would notice us or interrupt.

"What are you thinking? You cannot sacrifice yourself on the off chance it might lead to finding these shitheads. You are better than that."

"What am I supposed to do? We're running out of ideas. We're out of leads, and those shitheads put a fucking clock on things."

"What are you talking about?" I watched him storm through the empty conference room like a bull in a china shop. "What clock, Michael?"

"Sam didn't tell you?"

"She told me you want to hang yourself out to dry on the off chance it might lead to catching them. I don't care what or who they threatened. You are not doing that."

"I don't want to. The thought never would have crossed my mind, but things are different now."

"What happened? You got stupid all of a sudden?" I blinked. "This is the entire reason why we can't work together."

"It's not about you, Lexie," he huffed. "It's about all of us. You didn't see Evans. That could have easily been Kemper, Hawking, Sanchez, Cruise, or you."

But I knew he didn't worry about everyone else the same way he worried about me. Once Preston said it, I knew it was true. "Promise me you're not going to do any dumbass things while we're together. If you do, we're done. Is that understood?"

"I won't let them hurt anyone else, and this is the only way I can think to stop them. We cut Kazinski loose and see where he goes and who he talks to. Then we grab them all."

"What if you're wrong? It'll tip our hand. The Skulls will retaliate even harder if they think we're trying to trap them. They attacked last night to goad the department into fucking up. They upped the stakes to put us on tilt and throw us off our game. If we don't follow procedure, if we cut corners, it'll come out, and they'll win. We can't have that. Evans deserves better." I stared at Michael. "I deserve better."

He glared at me. "It's not that simple. Sam had no right to worry you with any of this, especially when she only gave you half the story."

"What do you mean?"

He reached into his jacket and pulled out a folded piece of paper, throwing it on the table in front of me.

I looked down at the sheet of paper.

"What choice do I have, Lexie? I'd rather lose my job than gamble with your life."

TWENTY-SIX

"We'll make an identification some other way. Kemper saw them. So did I. We'll get them. Just give it time," I said.

Michael stared down at the scrap of paper. "That'll take too long. They put us on a clock."

"So what? We make them wait."

"Funny, every time I've told you to be patient, you've gotten annoyed."

"That was different."

"How?" He sucked in a breath. "I'm not fighting with you on this, Lexie. This is a direct threat against the entire department, but specifically it's aimed at you. I won't have it."

"Think about it. We are talking about thieves and killers. I don't doubt for one second they aren't also liars. It's not like they have any idea how to find me. This is bullshit. They're just trying to scare us. Where did you even get this stupid piece of paper?"

"This is a copy. The original was pressed into Officer Evans' palm. He had a death grip on it. A nurse found it when they were prepping him for surgery."

Release Kazinski in the next forty-eight hours and stop hunting us or we'll kill Officer Bitch and anyone else in uniform. In case there was any question about their intended target, they scrawled my badge number beside it.

"They had your ID and badge. They know your name. How many Alessandra Sarconi's can there be in the city?" Michael asked.

"More than you'd think," I joked. But I may have been the only one. "They're not gonna find me, but let them try. I have the home court advantage and a loaded Glock. Tell them to bring it."

"I don't want them in the same time zone as you." His expression softened, and he stroked my cheek. He knew I was putting on a brave face, but he didn't shatter the illusion I was constructing. "We have to let Kazinski go. Jack doesn't want to give in to their demands. No one in the department does, but we should."

"This is why you're so sure Kazinski connects to them, unless that's another ploy. Maybe they want to distract and confuse us. While we look into him and his connections, they can do whatever they want."

"Which is why everyone else should stay the course and I'll follow Kazinski."

"You've never broken the rules before. You can't start now."

"Maybe you don't know me as well as you think."

"Michael?"

He shook his head. "I know where the line is. I've been on the right side of it ever since I pinned on the badge."

"Great, so you know how far over the line this is."

"I won't let them hurt you."

"Then find another way."

But the determined look in his eye was a dead giveaway that he'd do whatever it took to protect me, even if it meant sacrificing himself and us in the process. "Come on. Jack's going to hold a briefing. We don't want to be late. People might get the wrong idea."

"As if every single person in gangs doesn't already know about us," I mumbled.

After returning to the gangs unit, Devereaux called Michael over to his desk to update him on something. Lightman was in the conference room, which he had dubbed the war room. Preston was nowhere in sight.

"Sarconi," Lightman jerked his head, waiting for me to enter, "there's been a new development."

"You mean the threat against me?"

"Yes. Since you're aware of the circumstances, I'm wondering what you think we should do."

"Follow the evidence. It'll eventually lead to the men responsible, and by that point, our case should be airtight."

"You don't think we should capitulate?"

"No, sir."

"That's just what I wanted to hear." He reached for my medical clearance. "You've done enough for today. Go home, and come back refreshed. I want you out from behind that desk as soon as possible. How's your partner doing?"

"Partner?" Was he seriously asking about Michael's state of mind?

"Officer Kemper. His injuries weren't as severe, but the men who attacked him had reason to believe he could be dead. Do you know if he's back at full capacity yet?"

"I don't know."

"Before you leave, I need you to find out."

"Yes, sir." But I didn't think Kemper would be on duty now. It was too early.

Before I made it five steps, Michael grabbed my elbow and pulled me back into the conference room.

"Jack," he said, "we brought in the two assholes Sarconi stopped that first night. We ran their prints. It turns out one of them used to work for Sunshine Security. The techs are running a comparison of Sunshine Security's employee files to the stills we pulled from the street cams. Since those two bozos have a connection and we saw them spray painting a cruiser, I'm thinking they may be the taggers we've been chasing."

"It's not possible. They were under surveillance when Cruise was attacked."

"Not if we're looking at more than one team."

"We already theorized about two teams," I whispered to Michael.

He turned to look at me. "I'm thinking we're looking at a lot more than two teams. The Skulls have weaponized every reserve member in their arsenal. If we cut them a deal, they'll talk."

"You're sure?" Lightman climbed to his feet.

"That's what they said." Michael exhaled. "If they cooperate, we should be able to scoop up the assholes who've been attacking our own. We won't have to cut Kazinski loose to remove the threat."

"Did you get the DA's office on board?" Lightman asked.

"I already made the call. An ADA is on the way. He'll look things over, and we'll go from there."

"Excellent." Lightman looked at me, confused why I was still in the room. "Sarconi, weren't you going to find out about Kemper?"

"Yes, sir." I moved toward the door.

"Kemper's on light duty. He's been assigned the front desk," Michael said before I made it out of the room. "What do you want with him, Jack?"

"Nothing, now that we got this."

Now that things were heating up, I wanted to stick

around, but the detectives didn't need me. Until my badge matched theirs, I remained a glorified gofer.

Instead, I called for a rideshare and waited near the front door. For the first time since that night in the liquor store, I felt relief. We'd get their names and this would finally be over.

On the way home, I kept checking for a tail. No one was following me. I asked the driver to make a quick stop at the drug store to pick up the scar cream the doctor recommended. Something about being inside the store freaked me out. Maybe it was the Sunshine Security decal on the window or all the things Michael had said to me when we were alone in the conference room.

Even after I was dropped off outside my apartment, I still couldn't shake the feeling. I surveyed the area, unzipped my purse, tucked my handgun into my jacket pocket, grabbed my bag, and headed inside at a fast clip.

I'd encountered those men twice. The first time was insult, the second time injury. There couldn't be a next time, even if I had argued with Michael about it. I checked my phone, but I didn't have any calls or texts. But it had only been an hour. It would take longer than that to negotiate the terms of the deal and get the necessary intel out of the two men we arrested.

Again, my mind went back to the Sunshine Security decal. My first thought had been the crimes involved an inside man. But that was only relevant to the break-ins, not the violent crimes, except in the case of Mr. Cline. He's the one thing that connected both, besides the note the unsub had left in Officer Evans' hand.

We were still missing something. I didn't know what, but there was a big piece of the puzzle we had yet to figure out. I hoped the gangs unit would get to the bottom of it. I hated to think what the unsubs planned to do to me if they didn't get what they wanted. Why did they want Kazinski released? Were they afraid of what he'd tell us? Or was it a trick, like I had said to Michael?

Unlocking my apartment door, I stepped inside and flipped the deadbolt and regular lock back in place. I spun and nearly jumped out of my skin.

"What's with the Fort Knox routine?" Amber asked. "And why didn't you ask me to pick up the cream on my way here?"

I clutched my chest and breathed a sigh of relief. "You scared me."

"Yeah, I picked up on that. Did you seriously not realize I'd stop by to see you?" She made her way across the room, brushing her fingers against the bandage. "I heard they took your stitches out when you went to get cleared."

"Isn't that privileged information?"

"I'm an administrator."

"That's an abuse of power."

"Pish." She took the tape off so she could see the wound. "The cuts closed nicely. That's a plus. I was afraid they'd have to leave the stitches in a few more days. Were they a bitch to remove?"

"Yep." I removed my hand from my jacket pocket before she noticed my gun.

She cocked her head to the side. "Lexie, what's a matter?"

"Nothing. Do you want dinner?"

"I can't. I'm supposed to be meeting Jay since you no longer need a babysitter." She dropped onto the couch. "How was your first day back at work?"

"Long."

"You look like you could use a nap. Tell me you didn't work more than half a day."

"More like a day and a half."

"Lex—"

I held up my hand. "We made progress. The two creeps who filed a complaint against me were arrested for spray painting a police car. They're connected to this. Right now, Michael's convincing them to give up the men who attacked me. This is almost over."

"That's great." But Amber didn't look any more convinced of that than I was. Where did that feeling of relief go? It had been so short-lived. Maybe I'd dreamt it.

"Yep." I stretched out on the couch beside her and yawned. "So how was your day?"

After listening to Amber for almost an hour, she left to meet her hot paramedic for drinks to celebrate my recovery. Amber would drink to celebrate pretty much anything. Usually, we'd meet for drinks to celebrate it being Wednesday.

I locked the door again and slumped back onto the couch, feeling the butt of my gun dig into my side. I removed it from my jacket and placed it on the coffee table while I contemplated how stupid it was to be worried. But it wasn't worry, exactly. It was more confusion. Like a piece was still missing.

But it shouldn't be. The crimes were connected. The men were connected. We weren't looking at two teams. We were looking at potentially dozens. It was all about revenge. The Skulls wanted to get even. They said they'd slaughter us, and at least two men intended to follow through on that threat. The one who shot Kemper, and the one who shot Evans and attacked me. The third member of their team, the beta, was the weak link. But were they the only ones who wanted to kill cops? What about the other, less severe attacks?

My head started to spin. This case was too big.

Even now, with things supposedly coming together, it still felt humongous.

Deciding I needed to do something to de-stress now that my head and body both ached, I filled the tub with hot water and bubbles, relieved that I didn't have to wrap my arm in plastic. Instead, I rested it on a towel on the ledge since it was still too soon to soak it.

When the phone rang, I was chest deep in bubbles. I grabbed a towel, wrapping it around my body, and hurried to grab my phone. It was Michael.

"Hey," I marched to the linen closet to grab a fresh towel, "what's going on?"

"We offered immunity if they cooperated. I'm not going to get into everything right now, but we'll be arresting the remaining members of the Skulls."

"What about the men who attacked us in the liquor store? Do you know who they are?"

"We got one name, so far. We're still putting a few things together."

"But you're closing in on who's responsible?"

"It looks like it."

"In that case, I have a tub full of bubbles. There's just one thing missing."

"You're not supposed to have wine yet," Michael said.

"I wasn't talking about wine. I was talking about you. Are you on your way? I'll keep the water warm for you."

"I think this is going to turn into another all-nighter. Can you manage without me?"

"You barely got any sleep last night."

"I know, but I'm okay. If you're not, I can—"

"I'm fine, Michael. Stop worrying. Frankly, we could use some time apart. You were getting really annoying, cooking dinner, bringing me snacks, allowing us to have an all night make-out session followed by breakfast in bed. Do you have any idea how irritating those things are?"

"You loved every minute. I guess I'll see you tomorrow. Promise you'll call if you need anything."

"I will."

"Good."

We disconnected, and I sunk back into the bathtub. I deserved a night to relax and do whatever I wanted. Mainly, I wanted to sleep, but I might eat some potato chips and watch a movie first.

In the middle of the night, my phone rang.

"Sarconi," I answered, knowing four a.m. phone calls were never good.

"We just brought in a suspect. We need you to identify him," Lightman said.

Why was he still at work? He should have left hours ago. He'd been at work for at least the last twenty-four hours. Maybe more. I understood why, but no one should work that much. It'd impair judgment and performance. Hopefully, he'd gone home for a few hours before returning. I had to assume Michael wasn't there and didn't know about this, or he would have been the one who called me, which made me wonder where he was since he wasn't asleep beside me.

"You want me there now?" I squeezed my eyes closed, hoping to get the headache to dissipate faster.

"No, next year," Lightman spat. "Of course now. Why would I call you in the middle of the night if I didn't mean now? You said you were ready to work, so get your ass down here."

"I'm on my way."

TWENTY-SEVEN

"Number four," I jerked my chin at the glass, "that's him."

"You're positive?" Lightman asked. "You barely caught a glimpse of this guy before he took off and your partner stupidly pursued. Shouldn't you have focused your attention on the two other men you were attempting to handcuff instead of some clown who ran past you?"

I gave Lightman a dirty look. "I'm positive."

"You didn't seem so positive when you were describing him to the sketch artist."

I couldn't explain it, but the moment I saw that asshole again, memories of him pulling the trigger on Kemper came to mind. "I'll bet he also has a bullet wound or graze on his back. Or are you going to tell me I have the wrong man?"

"I'm not saying that. I'm just wondering why you couldn't recall these details sooner."

"Ease up, Jack," Preston said. "You know it's not that easy."

"It should have been."

"If you don't believe me," I continued, irritated because the tiny voice in the back of my head agreed with Lightman, "why don't you ask Kemper if he recognizes him?" I glared at the man through the two-way glass.

"We already did," Preston said. "Kemper picked out the same guy you did. We just wanted to make sure."

"Yeah, well, that's him. Now do what you have to in order to get him to give up the other two assholes." It was almost six a.m. I was exhausted and pissed.

"We will." Preston put a gentle hand on my shoulder and looked at Lightman. "Jack, why don't you put him in a room before Sarconi leaves? We don't need him to see her."

Lightman muttered something about not having to take orders from the two of us and continued out the door. He would have done it anyway. He just didn't like someone else suggesting it.

"Was a lineup really necessary?" I asked. "I'm a police officer. I've been trained to remember details."

"I know, but we're doing things by the book. Every T is getting crossed. The DA's office doesn't want to risk it after all the trouble they had to go through for us to get the intel to bring this guy in."

"I wish you'd gotten the name of his two accomplices. I'm sure Officer Evans would agree."

"We'll get him to give them up. It's just a matter of time. Our two graffiti artists didn't know their names, but they described the guy who shot Evans and cut you as one scary SOB. We have decent sketches. And now that we have Curtis Ross in custody, we can squeeze him for the intel."

"Curtis Ross?"

"The man you just IDed. He doesn't have a chance in hell of walking. It'd be in his best interest to cooperate."

"He intended to kill Kemper. We need to nail him to the wall."

"We will. We may have let the other two yahoos

walk since spray paint is one thing. But attempted murder of a police officer isn't even in the same universe. It'd be like comparing apples to elephants. Correction, apples to inorganic compounds."

Either I was really tired, or Preston had lost her mind. More than likely, it was a little bit of both.

She lowered her voice. "Hey, thanks for speaking to Michael. I was afraid he'd do something reckless." Her smile was bittersweet. "He must really love you."

"Where is he?"

"Jack sent us all home at eight. He wasn't planning on calling any of us back in, but I heard what was going on and came in to help." She looked through the glass at the now empty room and opened the door. "You should go home and get some sleep. We'll call you if we need anything else."

On my way out, Kemper caught up to me. "Lexie, they called you too? How are you? Should you even be here? I thought you needed to rest."

"I'm fine. I've been cleared for light duty, which means we won't be riding together for a while."

"You mean you'd still ride with me? You forgive me?"

"It was a mistake." I met his eyes. "Don't make another one."

"Did you get my flowers? I wanted to send something else, but I didn't know what you'd like."

"There was no need," I began, but he silenced me with a wave of his hand.

"So you and Detective Riley?"

I gave him an icy glare, daring him to say it. "What about me and Detective Riley?"

"Nothing."

I stepped away. "I'll see ya later."

"See ya."

As we parted ways, I couldn't help but wonder if

the whole department knew Michael Riley and I were dating. Shaking it away to deal with later, since one crisis at a time was more than enough, I left the station.

Preston said Detective Lightman sent everyone home at eight. But when I spoke to Michael, he said they'd be working through the night. Maybe things had changed and he'd gone home, believing me when I said we needed to spend some time apart, but I didn't think that's what was going on here. So I called him.

"Hey, Lexie." He sounded exhausted. "Is everything okay?"

"Where are you?"

"I'm at work."

"Bullshit. I'm at the station. Try again."

"Are you checking up on me?"

I fought the urge to say something I'd regret. "Tell me where you are."

"I'm staking out Kazinski's shop. Since the note they left said we had to release Kazinski, they must be waiting for him for a reason. I figured they'd show up here."

"Maybe they went to his house instead."

"Frank's got that covered."

"Does Lightman know what you're doing?" I asked.

"He's aware."

Turning the key in the ignition, I put the phone on speaker so I could search for Kazinski's shop and enter the address into my GPS. Once I saw where it was, I pulled out of the parking space.

"I'm coming to you." I hung up before he could protest. Luckily, Michael didn't try to call back. Maybe he knew better than to argue with me.

When I arrived, I spotted his car parked at the end of the street. I parked behind him and looked around.

I didn't see anyone nearby, so I got out of my car. Michael unlocked the doors, and I got in on the passenger side.

"Curtis Ross is in custody. He's the man who shot Kemper."

"The one that you winged?" Michael asked, and I nodded. "Do we have a solid case against him?"

"Lightman didn't tell me much, but Kemper and I were both able to pick him out of a lineup. Lightman put him in the box. He's going to squeeze until he gives up his two buddies."

"And Jack didn't think that could wait until a decent hour?" Michael stifled a yawn, shifting in his seat.

"You wouldn't have wanted to wait either." I peered out the windshield. "Has there been any activity?"

"No, but I may have blinked out for a few minutes around two a.m. I'm not really sure."

I ran my hand against his cheek, surprised when he nuzzled against it. "What do you think you're going to accomplish by being here?"

"I have to stop them. This can't happen again."

"Michael, look at me."

Reluctantly, he tore his eyes away from the windshield. "We've arrested one of them. We're still gathering evidence. A million things are in the works. You need to go home and get some sleep. I need you sharp, tiger, especially if you end up going against them. I've seen what they can do firsthand. Kemper and I were on high alert. We thought we were prepared, that we could handle it, and we couldn't. I'm sure Evans thought the same thing." But he wouldn't budge. "Do you want to risk Frank's safety on some stupid hunch?"

That got to him. Picking up his phone, he called Frank, updated him on the arrest, and said he thought they should call it a night. He put the phone down and looked at me. "You win."

"I wasn't trying to win."

"Come home with me," he said. "It's the only way I'll be able to sleep without worrying."

"I'll follow you."

He squeezed my hand before letting me out of the car.

TWENTY-EIGHT

"All right, everyone, listen up." Lightman stabbed at two photos tacked to the board. "These men are considered armed and dangerous. As far as we know, they're responsible for putting three of our own in the hospital and killing that jewelry store owner." Lightman picked up copies of the dossier he'd made and passed them out. "This man," he indicated the one with the neck tattoo, "is Zachary Shaw. He's Adan Shaw's cousin. Until now, he's kept off our radar, but according to Curtis Ross, Zachary's accomplice, Zachary's always been an integral part of the Skulls. When Adan got pinched, Zachary continued to run things behind the scenes. Consider him upper management. He was never on the front lines, which is why we never spotted him during any of our surveillance missions or when we've busted members of the gang for illegal activity. He stays in the background and gets the hell out before we even get close. But from the things Curtis has said, this guy is the lowest level of low. He's raped. He's killed. He's a fucking sadist and greedy as hell."

"Meaning?" Devereaux asked.

"Zachary put the break-ins into motion. His fence, Kazinski, was willing to pay top dollar for gold and jewelry. That's why they chose most of the locations they did. The other places they hit were mostly cash businesses. But it wasn't just about the money. He wanted to lure us to these locations to pick us off one by one."

"Or two by two," Michael muttered.

Lightman ignored the comment. "We've brought Adan Shaw in for questioning. He's denied his involvement, but since his cousin has mostly targeted businesses protected by Sunshine Security, we should assume Adan fed him the information he needed on the systems and how to avoid detection and how to attract a lot of attention. It's also possible someone else with ties to Sunshine provided this information. We know one of the taggers used to work for Sunshine. For all we know, the whole outfit is dirty, but I'm not banking on that. We're holding Adan as long as we possibly can before cutting him loose. The more of their men we take off the board, the better."

"Who's been spray painting the Skulls' symbol on the walls?" I asked.

"According to Curtis Ross, the tag was to be used by everyone assisting the Skulls."

"How many vandals are we looking at?" Devereaux asked.

"At last count, the Skulls had eight men who remained free, but another fifteen in what we've called the reserves. Most of them have this neck tattoo." Lightman pointed to an enlarged photo. "But not all of them do, which makes it harder to identify them. However, we currently believe only Zachary Shaw and," he flicked the second photo, "Anthony Hawley have the primary objective of murdering any and every police officer they find. But don't let your guard down. If the opportunity presents itself, every other member of the Skulls won't hesitate to take a shot at us. Ask Officers Hawking, Sanchez, and Cruise about that."

"The trace we performed on the prepaid credit card came back," Preston said. "We located the store where the card was purchased and have surveillance footage which shows Shaw and Ross making the purchase. That's our proof they bought the burner, made the call, and set us up. Couple that with Ross's statement, and we have enough to lock them up for decades."

"We just have to find these bastards," Michael muttered.

"Anthony Hawley may be your weak link," I said.

Lightman looked as if he was unsure if he should ignore me or ask more questions. Finally, he sighed. "Why do you say that?"

I repeated what I'd already told Michael. "Maybe he was afraid they'd get caught."

"Or maybe he's not good with the violence." Preston reached for the ballistics report. "He could have been the shooter in the alley. The one who fired into the dumpster instead of directly into Kemper."

"I still don't know how many men were waiting to ambush us, but the area wasn't very large. It couldn't have been more than two, but maybe it was just Hawley," I said.

Lightman flipped through one of the folders. "He doesn't have a record. Curtis Ross said Hawley was involved, that he does a lot of planning and logistics for the Skulls, but he didn't go into any specifics. But the taggers we released didn't know anything about him. They supposedly didn't even know his name."

"He could be a non-violent offender. The moneyman, so to speak," Devereaux suggested.

"Or he could be just a tad smarter and more aware of the consequences," Michael said. "He could be the one who gave us a deadline to release Kazinski. The best thing for Hawley would be to put some money together and get out of town."

"It doesn't matter either way," Lightman said. "We know who they are. We're going to stop them. In the meantime, we've made more sweeping arrests. Search warrants are to follow, and we'll make sure charges stick to every single one of these shitheads. They brought this upon themselves." After Lightman gave us our marching orders, he dismissed us.

I returned to the desk at the back of the bullpen. But one thing bothered me.

Michael casually put a bottle of water down beside me before heading for the double doors. He and Preston were told to brief the watch commander so patrol would know what was going on.

When he returned, I waved him over, pretending to need help getting one of the search warrants. "I've been thinking about it, and the only way Zachary and Anthony Hawley would know Mr. Cline was assisting us is if Adan, or someone else in Sunshine Security told them. If not, how could they know the jewelry store owner was cooperating with us on the investigation?"

"You think Adan watched the whole thing?"

"I do. He probably saw us arrive and leave. That's how they knew when to strike."

"That fits with our previous theory and everything we've been saying. But unless someone talks, we have no evidence to dig deeper. The judge already said family ties weren't enough."

"They should be."

"Hey," Michael called, "can I take a stab at Curtis Ross and Adan Shaw?"

Lightman didn't look happy. "I'll go with you. You can fill me in on the way."

"Actually, it was Sarconi's idea," Michael said.

"Maybe she could sit in instead."

"We're not doing that on this. She's going to testify against Ross as both a cop and a victim." Lightman pointed at me. "You're staying here."

I never wanted anything different. "Yes, sir."

When Riley and Lightman returned an hour later, Lightman summoned me into the conference room and closed the door. "Your hunch may be correct, but Adan Shaw sure as shit won't say anything other than he's innocent, and Ross won't admit to anything else. He gave us his accomplices, but he won't say or do anything that will incriminate him further. He says the other two chose the locations. He had nothing to do with it."

"What about the alley? Did you ask about that?"

"He says he wasn't there."

"Was Hawley?"

"Do I look like a search engine?"

"Only when you have a blank stare." Unable to stop the smartass remark from leaving my lips, I grimaced. "Sorry, sir. It's the concussion."

"Be that as it may," Lightman growled, "I didn't call you in here to answer your questions. I wanted to know if you were up for some decoy work."

"Decoy work?" He couldn't seriously be thinking of sending me back to vice. "Medical's only cleared me for desk duty."

"Light duty," he corrected. "I'm not asking you to do anything physically taxing. But as you know, that clock these pricks put us on has run out. Besides a few minor incidents while we made the arrests, no violent attacks have been reported. However, Ross insists that will change if Zachary Shaw doesn't get what he wants. So we're thinking of letting Kazinski walk out of here. We'll monitor his movements and see what happens, but we're thinking of feeding him a few details about you before we let him go. That way, if Shaw and Hawley decide to follow through, which Ross assures us they will since that was their plan all along, we'll have the trap set."

"I'm the bait."

"If you prefer that term."

I barely survived my last encounter. But I couldn't let this happen again. I promised myself we'd get these guys when I learned Cline was killed. And that was before these assholes went after me and my friends. "What do you want me to do?"

Lightman smiled. "That's exactly what I like to hear."

~*~

"How are you doing in there?" Michael asked.

I looked around the cheap motel room. "At least they have cable."

"Just remember, the department is not going to pay for any adult programming. So don't get any funny ideas."

"If I wanted adult entertainment, I'd ask you to strip."

He laughed. "What makes you think I'd do that?"

"Are you saying you wouldn't?"

"I'm saying I'd want you to return the favor."

I moved to the window and peered outside. Devereaux and Riley were in a room directly across the parking lot from me. With only one way in and out, if Zachary Shaw or any of his minions wanted to make a move on me, we'd see them coming a mile away.

"Tit for tat."

He snickered. "I like the sound of that."

"Let's get out of this mess first." I moved away from

the window and turned on the TV.

Kazinski had been released a few hours ago. A surveillance team was tailing him. So far, he'd gone to his shop and made a few calls. We had his phone tapped. One of the numbers he dialed was to Shaw's burner. All he said was he was out and after they made the final exchange, he wanted no part of any of this. We had eyes on the usual places we suspected they might meet, but so far, no one had shown.

"Try to get some sleep," Michael said. "You may be back at work, but you're supposed to be taking it easy."

"How can I sleep when two men are planning to kill me?"

"Frank and I are right outside. We're not going to let that happen."

"If it's all the same to you, I'd prefer to stay sharp."

"Fine, but it could be hours or days."

"Let's hope not." I exhaled, hanging up.

The nervous energy coursed through me. But I'd been in enough situations like this to know the suspects would most likely be picked up before they ever got anywhere near me. They'd have to get the intel from Kazinski since he hadn't told them a thing over the phone.

After pacing until my legs hurt, I climbed onto the bed and stared out the slit in the blinds. But there was no movement in the parking lot. Propping myself up against several pillows, I turned on the TV and flipped until I found an animated film.

Three hours later, Michael called back. "Jack phoned. He said they saw action. Two men are in custody now. They met Kazinski at the park to collect the money. Jack and Sam saw the exchange. When they intercepted, they came under fire. Both men were shot. Sam thought she saw someone else fleeing the scene. Regardless, we're calling it."

"Are they dead?" I asked.

"They are on their way to the hospital now. I'm going to help work the scene. Frank will give you a ride back to the station."

I turned off the TV and climbed off the bed. "But we got Shaw and Hawley?"

Michael hesitated. "They didn't have any IDs with them. The injuries they sustained made it a little hard to ID them from the photos, but Jack said one of them had a broken nose, black eyes, and a swollen face. The other, well, let's just say Officer Evans wasn't the only one who ended up disfigured."

After grabbing my gun and making sure I didn't leave anything else behind, I opened the door to find Devereaux waiting outside.

"Are you ready to go?" he asked.

"Yep." I nodded to Michael, who was across the parking lot, getting into his car, and got in beside Frank.

TWENTY-NINE

Since I had nothing to do with any of this, Lt. Peterson told me to go home. My union rep would not be happy about the long hours or learning I'd been asked to play decoy, not that I planned to tell him. But Peterson didn't want any problems. So I left without another word.

Normally, I parked in the back which was where Kemper was heading. He grinned and bumped against my shoulder. "I heard the news. Gangs believes they caught the assholes who tried to kill us."

"I know."

He gave me a sideways look. "Were you there?"

"Not exactly."

He shook his head. "For someone who said she wanted to keep her head down, you're sure showing a lot of initiative. You just want to outdo me."

"That wasn't my intention, but these shitheads made it personal."

"That they did."

"Hey, Bobby," someone called, "do you have a minute?"

Kemper stopped and turned. "Yeah. What's up?"

"Good night," I said.

"Night? Jeez, Lexie, look outside. It's practically

morning."

I exited through the front door and got into my car. Normally, I parked in the back lot, but since I'd been working weird hours, I had found somewhere else to park. Luckily, none of my overzealous colleagues had decided to ticket or tow me. Taking a deep breath, I told myself this was over and pulled into early morning traffic. I'd forgotten how obnoxious rush-hour could be, particularly when the roads were filled with sleep deprived, caffeine-addled people late for work. In a few days, I'd be one of them. Today, I was only sleep deprived, and my warm bed was calling my name.

I scanned for a possible tail, but in the early morning hours with the sun barely breaching the horizon and an endless sea of vehicles surrounding me, I didn't see anything out of the ordinary. Thirty minutes later, I parked outside my apartment building, bending over the center console to grab my purse from where it had fallen off the passenger's seat.

Without warning, my window shattered, spraying glass everywhere. I turned, seeing an aluminum bat swinging toward me. I threw myself over the console, opening the passenger's side door. I tumbled out of the car, unzipping my bag and removing my gun as I fought to gain my footing and get up.

A hand reached into the driver's side window and unlocked the door. He opened the door and leaned in, surprised to find the interior empty. I kicked the passenger's side door closed as he dove across the seats to get me. *Zachary Shaw.* I recognized the ugly ink peeking out over his collar. That asshole carved the message into my forearm, and now he was back to finish the job.

How did he survive? The thought raced through my mind as I skittered backward, finally getting my feet underneath me. With my gun in hand, I fixed my stare on the car, waiting for even the slightest movement. He wouldn't get away this time.

Something shifted in the shrubbery near my building, and I turned, afraid Hawley or someone else was lurking in the shadows, waiting to blindside me again. No one was there, but in those few milliseconds, the car door cracked open.

"Police, freeze," I said before firing a shot that shattered the passenger's side window and whizzed past his head, lodging in the roof of my car.

Shaw laughed, that awful sound I had heard while I had lain in utter agony inside the liquor store. "You missed." He slipped back out the driver's side, placing my car between us. The only weapon I could see was a bat, but that didn't mean he didn't have a gun or knife.

I kept my gun trained on his position, realizing he wanted me to expel my entire clip. But I didn't have a good angle or a clear shot. My cell phone was beside the car with the rest of the spilled items from my purse, so I couldn't call for backup.

Going against every bit of training and protocol that had been programmed into me, I calculated the distance to my apartment building, fired another warning shot to distract him, and ran as fast as I could in the opposite direction. I had to get inside. I needed backup or a clear shot. This was my best chance.

Someone must have heard the shots and called 9-1-1, and if no one had, I made sure someone would by running through the lobby, screaming. But no one poked a head out to see about the commotion.

I was searching for a defensible position when he caught me. He grabbed my hair, pulling me backward. I stumbled, falling to the ground. Turning, I squeezed the trigger again, grazing him with my wild shot. He howled, swinging the bat. Pain shot through my arm, and my gun clattered to the floor, some distance away.

"You fucking bitch." He pressed his palm into his shoulder, pulling his hand away to find it red with blood. "I'm gonna paint these walls with you."

He swung again, and I dove to the side, hearing the echoing clang of the aluminum bat against the hard tile floor.

"It won't matter. We know who you are. So smile pretty for the camera. It's right behind you," I pointed, hoping to distract him.

Automatically, he looked in the direction I indicated, and I kicked him hard in the sternum, sending him sprawling backward. I raced toward my gun, but he grabbed my ankle.

I hit the ground hard. White hot pain went through me, sending a cascade of fire through my head. For a moment, I thought I'd black out.

My instincts took over, and I kicked my free leg backward, the ball of my foot connecting with his upper chest and neck. He made a choking sound and let me go.

I flipped around to face him, but I couldn't find my footing to get off the ground. Instead, I slid backward, digging my heels into the tile and pushing off to put as much distance between us as possible. My gun was nowhere in sight. I needed a weapon. I needed something.

He laughed, lifting the discarded bat and moving slowly toward me. He cleared the distance between us in no time. I desperately searched for my gun, but it was across the lobby, out of reach.

Shifting into a fighting stance, I hoped to shield myself from the blows. If I could get in close enough, maybe I could fight. We'd learned self-defense in the academy, and while he was bigger and stronger, I wasn't above fighting dirty. I'd make him cry or die trying.

He swung, and I braced for the impact, my eyes closing automatically. But the hit didn't come. Instead, I heard flesh hitting flesh, and the bat clanged to the floor. I opened my eyes. My attacker was on the ground. Michael was on top of him, throwing punch after punch. Once the assailant was dazed, Michael flipped him over and cuffed him.

"Lexie," he said, intensely focused on the man beneath him, "are you okay?"

"Uh-huh," I gasped, collecting my gun and aiming it at the downed man.

Sirens sounded, and half a dozen police officers burst through the front door of my apartment building. While four of them dealt with the man leaving a pool of blood on the beige tile, someone else took the gun from my shaking hand. Seconds later, Michael hugged me tightly, one hand on the back of my head, the other arm wrapped around me.

"How did you know?" I asked against his neck.

"Jack called me as soon as he realized the man that was shot wasn't Shaw. The other man wasn't Hawley either. They were two lowlifes. I was on my way to the station when I spotted Hawley going after Kemper." Michael gulped down some air.

"Is he—"

"He's fine. We stopped the guy in time, but this asshole gave us the slip. I knew he'd come after you. I tried calling, but you didn't pick up." He watched the officers bustle about, calling paramedics to the scene. They requested two ambulances. One for me and one for the man who wanted me dead. I clung tighter to Michael. "Are you sure you're okay, Lexie?"

He eased out of my grip, keeping a steadying hand on my waist. He studied my eyes and ran a hand along the sides of my face and neck. My temple hurt from where I'd hit the ground, but it wasn't bleeding. Carefully, he lifted my swollen arm with a trembling hand. A large welt had erupted where the bat had made contact. My arm might have been broken. I wasn't sure.

He held me sideways against him. "Relax. It's the adrenaline rush. I think you're okay, but I don't want you to pass out. Slow, deep breaths, okay?"

"You're the one shaking."

He barked some things at the responding officers. Until someone else showed up to take charge, this was Michael's scene.

I pushed away from him. "I'm okay. That bastard isn't taking anything else from me."

Michael nodded, understanding that I wasn't about to jeopardize our careers for a few comforting seconds in his arms.

I moved to the staircase and took a seat on the bottom step, cradling my arm against my side. Five minutes later, Preston arrived with another detective I didn't recognize.

Preston sent two uniforms with the paramedics to escort the handcuffed killer to the hospital. His injuries weren't that severe. Michael had restrained himself, which surprised me since I had wanted to pull that trigger.

"I'm surprised he's still breathing," she said.

Michael stared at the ceiling and shook his head. "Death would be too good for him. Plus, I made someone a promise. I didn't want to break it." He winked at me.

"Jack will be happy about that. We still have the mess with the Skulls to figure out." Preston sat down beside me, signaling for the second team of EMTs. "Tell me what happened while they get you patched up."

I gave her the play-by-play. My car, the shots I fired, the ensuing fight, and Michael rushing in to save the day. "How's Kemper?" Michael said he was fine, but since they didn't exactly get along, it wouldn't hurt to get a second opinion.

"He got a little banged up, about the same as you. Nothing too bad. He's lucky Michael showed up when he did. If he hadn't gotten to the station at that exact moment, things might be different." She looked around the bloody lobby. "I saw your car. This attack was brutal."

"Agreed."

Michael leaned against the wall beside me, his arms folded over his chest, his hands tucked away to hide the tremors. I wasn't the only one dealing with the adrenaline dump. "We'll get forensics to check it out." He gestured to two officers. "Rope everything off. Make sure no one contaminates our scene. I want this guy to go away for every single crime he's ever committed. I don't care if we're talking class D misdemeanors for littering. I want everything we have on him, so no evidence gets compromised and no scene gets contaminated."

"Yes, sir." The two officers went outside while another two looked around the lobby of my building.

Preston snickered when Michael walked away to speak to the other detective who had shown up. "After saving Kemper, he tore through the station, wanting to know where you were and if you were safe. Before any of us even had time to ask a question, he was in his car on the way here. I was right behind him, but it's a good thing he didn't wait."

The EMT manipulated my arm around, and I hissed.

"X-rays might be in order, Officer," he said. "Do

you want a ride to the hospital?"

"I want to finish up here first," I said.

"We have it covered." Preston dismissed the man. "I'll finish taking your statement on the way. We'll get the paperwork signed, and you should be home in time for lunch."

"I'm just glad it's over."

She gave me a look. "It's not over yet."

THIRTY

"This sucks," I pouted. The hospital was concerned that the recent smack to the head might have done more damage, so I was out for the next few days to make sure that didn't happen again.

"The doctor said no physical exertion for the next forty-eight hours. That was an intense ordeal. You need to be careful. You don't want to risk brain damage." Michael brushed his lips against mine. He ran his fingers along the brace on my arm. "You're lucky you don't need a cast."

"It's only a hairline fracture. I'm perfectly fine. I've never been better."

He gave me a *yeah, right* look.

"Seriously, I'm okay. The headache comes and goes, but everything else is back to normal." Giving up against his stubborn, unyielding nature, I edged my pillow closer to him and settled down in the soft bedding. "Are you going to tell me what happened with the case?"

"We got them all and enough evidence to make sure Zachary Shaw goes away for the next few decades. Hawley's hoping to cut a deal, but he'll be serving hard time. I'll make sure of that."

"He tried to kill Kemper twice," I said.

Michael nodded. "Yeah, he's the shooter from the alley. Shaw made him do it. He wanted Hawley to prove he wasn't a pussy and was just as committed to their vendetta."

"I'm glad it was Hawley and not Shaw in that alley, or we wouldn't have survived."

Michael looked away. He didn't want to think about it.

"Do we know if Adan Shaw tipped his cousin off that Mr. Cline was assisting?"

"We don't know for sure," Michael said. "We subpoenaed the phone records and all of Adan's other methods of communication, along with Sunshine Security's records. We haven't found anything for sure, but if we do, Jack's prepared to throw the book at Adan too."

"At least we got the men who killed Cline." I still regretted not being able to prevent that from happening.

"How about you ask Amber when she wants to go on that double date? You could use some cheering up, and I've earned a day off after all this OT."

"Do you really think that's a good idea?"

"We can't stop living our lives because of this."

"That's not what I meant."

"Sweetie, I promise no one else is going to get hurt because we're out on a date. Just don't spread it around that I'm a nice guy, or you'll ruin my street cred." He kissed my cheek, and I chuckled. "We have a lot to celebrate, and I don't want to waste a single moment that could be spent with you."

"Me neither." I rested my head against his shoulder as he played with my hair.

~*~

The next morning, the lieutenant requested Michael stop by the station.

"Can I come with you?" I asked. "I was there. I have a right to know what's going on."

"I'm sure the LT will follow up with you too, but you should wait for him to call. In the meantime, make sure you have the details straight. You discharged your weapon several times. Someone's going to ask about it."

"Shaw tried to kill me. He would have killed me."

"But he didn't have a gun. You did. That could make things dicey."

"He killed Evans. No one's going to bat an eye, Michael."

He smiled. "Which explains why you feared for your life or why you used excessive force."

"Do you think it was excessive? He would have killed me."

"Lexie," Michael took my face in his hands, "I'm only saying this to prepare you. You know how IAD is. They like to make a lot of accusations, but everyone from parking patrol to the top level brass knows exactly what the Skulls planned to do to us. More than likely, you'll get a commendation for your bravery."

"Unless they say I screwed up."

"You didn't, but I don't want you to get blindsided either." He kissed my lips gently, breaking away and tracing my bottom lip with his thumb. "You did what you had to." He closed his eyes and leaned back. "I should have found a way to stop them sooner."

"That's not your job."

"It was my case. That makes it my job."

I rolled my eyes. "Fine, but yesterday morning, you saved my life. The only reason I'm here is because of you, and tonight, I intend to show you exactly how grateful I am. Do not for one second blame yourself for not getting here sooner. You were here when it mattered." I clasped his face in my hands and rested my forehead against his. "You've always been there when I needed you the most, and I know you always will be." I swallowed. "Thanks for keeping your word."

"Does that mean you think we can work together?"

"I guess it does. But that's not my call. It's Lightman's."

Michael smiled. "Good, because he's already on board. He wouldn't have given you a desk in gangs if he wasn't planning on keeping you around."

"Did you make that happen?"

He pressed his lips together and nodded. "You asked me to. It's not my fault if Jack thought I meant permanently."

"He knows," I said. "Everyone does. We're going to have to disclose. Once it's official, he may change his mind."

"He won't, but let's wait until after you get the exam results back. Jack's cool with a lot of things, but not everyone in charge is."

"Copy," I said.

Michael gave me another kiss and got up. "I have to go. I'll be back later."

"Be careful."

Once he was gone, I took an unsteady breath, cleaned up our breakfast dishes, and phoned Amber to make plans for our double date night. IAD would want my statement, but worrying and second-guessing myself would just make me crazy. So this was a much more enjoyable use of my brain power.

Later that afternoon, two internal affairs investigators stopped by my apartment to ask questions about the night of the original attack. I hated having to explain what happened again, but they wanted to review those facts before moving on to what transpired yesterday morning.

"The shooting looks clean, Officer Sarconi. You had

every reason to fear for your life. Not only did Zachary have a bat, but he also had a knife on him. He planned to hurt you. You had every reason to defend yourself through any means necessary. He was bigger, stronger, and not saddled with the injuries you had sustained during the previous attack. We believe firing your weapon was appropriate under the circumstances."

"That's because it was."

"How did Detective Riley know Zachary Shaw would strike when he did? One of your neighbors called 9-1-1, but Riley left the station before the call was routed through dispatch."

"Riley's an excellent detective. From what I was told, he arrived at the station around the same time Hawley was making an attempt on Officer Kemper's life. It didn't take much to piece the two together." I shrugged. "I don't care how he figured it out. I'm just glad he showed up when he did. Why haven't you asked him about that?"

"We have." The investigator smiled, almost winking, unless I was hallucinating. "You have yourself a good day, Officer Sarconi. We'll be in touch."

After they left, I dialed my partner. Kemper assured me he was fine. I told him what I knew about the criminals and the reason we were targeted. It really wasn't his fault. It was just shitty luck.

During our call, I got a beep. Amber wanted to make sure I was feeling up to going out tonight. She didn't know what happened yesterday, and I didn't tell her. Instead, I promised Michael and I would meet her and her new beau, Jay, for dinner and drinks.

Disconnecting, I dialed Michael and left a message. By the time I put the phone down, I felt like a telephone operator. Maybe that was the alternative career path I should have taken.

Laughing at the thought, I hopped into the shower, glad to be free to lather up without risk of wetting my stitches or brace since I had taken it off before stepping under the spray. The swelling in my arm had already decreased, and I had a full range of motion. It just hurt to make a fist or lift heavy objects.

Two hours later, Michael unlocked my apartment door and came inside with a garment bag over his arm and an overnight bag slung over his shoulder. I was sitting in the living room, watching TV, dressed for our date with Amber and Jay. He smiled and kissed me.

"You look beautiful. Just give me a minute to change, and we'll get going. I hope my overnight bag isn't overstepping any of our boundaries since you said you thought we needed to spend less time together."

"When are you going to let that go?" I asked.

"Never."

I leaned back to watch him change through the open bedroom door. "It's cute you think I'm letting you stay the night."

"Is that how you show your gratitude?" he asked, recalling my words from this morning. "And to think I was planning to buy you dinner."

"Really? You think I'm that easy?" I stood when he came into the living room dressed in a black suit with a blue shirt that matched his eyes and a black tie. "Damn. Forget dinner. You can take me now."

"In that case, you should be offering to buy me dinner." He ran a hand down the brace on my arm. "It hasn't been forty-eight hours yet."

"No, but it'll be thirty-six by the time we get home. And I will burst into flames if you make me wait another twelve hours."

He smirked, an arrogant, self-assured look that was a million different kinds of sexy. "I'm a cop, not a firefighter."

"God, why do I have the urge to make a very dirty hose joke?"

"We better get going. With the mood you're in, we could use a chaperone." He leaned in, his breath caressing my ear as he said, "And I'm two seconds away from peeling that dress off of you." He stepped back, winking. He held my coat out, guiding it onto me before giving my ass a playful swat. "Thirty-six it is."

THIRTY-ONE

Dinner with Amber could have gone better. Unfortunately, I was the universe's punching bag. The paramedic that treated my arm was the same paramedic my best friend was seeing, and instead of playing along with my act that we'd never met, he told her about the call he responded to the previous morning.

"Lexie," she sighed, "when are you going to take my advice?"

"I'm not." I narrowed my eyes, silently communicating that she drop it. "So how long has this been going on?" I gestured between the two of them.

"Three weeks." Jay launched into some cutesy story about first meeting Amber at the vending machine.

While he spoke, Amber and I engaged in a silent battle of wills. Unfortunately, my best friend never knew when to keep her mouth shut. "Jay, babe, can you get us another round of drinks from the bar? Make sure Lexie's is a virgin."

Michael snorted, and I dug my fingernails into his thigh.

"On second thought, get a bottle for the table," she gave Michael a saccharine grin, "since most of us are able to drink."

"Sure, no problem." Jay dutifully excused himself.

"Should I leave too?" Michael asked. "Or do I need to go to the car and grab my stun gun?" He had seen Amber and me fight before and could sense it was coming.

"Don't move an inch, Riley," she hissed. "Why didn't you tell me what happened?"

"Because it's over. I'm okay. Michael saved me." My voice softened, and I leaned into him. "Please don't ruin our night. The last thing I want is to think about this."

Amber seemed like she was about to protest, so Michael cleared his throat. "Amber," he warned, his voice hard, "no."

She shifted her gaze from him to me. "Fine," she pointed a finger at Michael, "but you better make sure you protect my girl. I don't know what I'd do without her."

"You have my word." He ran his hand through my hair. "I don't know what I'd do without her either."

Jay returned to the table, putting the wine bottle and fresh set of glasses down. "What did I miss?"

"Nothing," I locked eyes with Michael, "but we're going to call it a night."

"Yeah," Michael said, stroking my hair. He spent another few seconds gazing into my eyes before looking at our friends. "It was nice to meet you, Jay." He extended his hand. "We'll have to do this again." He reached into his wallet and laid some cash on the table. "Enjoy the wine. It's my treat." He smiled at Amber. "Thanks for always taking such good care of Lexie."

"Obviously, someone has to," she said, "but you do a decent enough job most of the time." She cracked a smile and stood up to hug me. "No more close calls," she whispered in my ear. "Promise?"

"I promise."

"Okay," she pulled me even closer, "and you were right about Riley dressing up."

~*~

Michael and I barely made it inside before his lips were on mine. We shut the door in a frenzy, attacking each other with fervent kisses. His hands were everywhere, and I hurriedly undid his tie, tossing it away. Something crashed to the ground, and Michael turned to see my table lamp had fallen victim to his balled-up tie.

"Timeout," he breathed, stepping away. "We either need to find a padded cell or we have to take this party into the bedroom."

"What?"

"There are far too many hard objects and sharp corners, and you've had a horrible string of luck lately, honey. I'll be there in a second. I have to get something out of my bag."

"Hurry," I grabbed his lapels and kissed him urgently, "flames, bursting, very bad."

He laughed, sliding the zipper of my dress down as soon as I turned around. I stepped out of my dress, leaving it on the floor in a heap. As soon as I stepped foot inside the bedroom, I slid my shoes off, leaving a trail of clothing on the way to the bed.

I lay back against the mattress, waiting for Michael. "What's taking so long?" I called, even if it had only been five seconds.

"I thought I should check to make sure your lamp wasn't broken or a potential fire hazard. All that talk of flames might have jinxed us."

"Is my apartment on fire?"

"No."

"Then get in here."

Michael came into the bedroom with his eyes hooded and a sexy grin on his face. "Are you sure you're okay?"

"Just don't bang my head against the headboard."

~*~

I woke up early. The sky was beginning to lighten, but the sun wasn't up yet. For the first time in days, I didn't have a headache. I studied the man next to me. So peaceful and strong. Safe, caring, and protective. How did I get so lucky?

He let out a contented sigh and curled closer to me. "Lexie," he whispered, "what are you doing?"

"Thinking about how lucky we are." I took a breath. "Michael?"

"Hmm?"

"I love you."

"I love you more."

THIRTY-TWO

The day of the detective's exam, Michael left my apartment without waking me. I was sleeping far more than normal, but hopefully, that would subside soon enough. It was the only residual symptom of the concussion. My arm was to remain in the brace for another week. Then I'd be back on duty too.

When I showed up to take the exam, I feared everything that had happened would be used against me, but the brass seemed impressed. I took a seat and waited to get started. By the time I walked out of the room, I felt confident I'd get promoted.

"How did it go?" Michael asked, catching up to me in the hallway.

"Good, I think. I don't know. I don't want to jinx it, but—"

"I'm sure you knocked it out of the park." He looked confused. "Where are you headed?"

"Lt. Peterson wants to see me."

Michael looked like he wanted to kiss me, but remembered where he was and refrained. "We'll catch up later, Officer Sarconi."

Before he could walk away, I said, "Hey, you were right. I don't want to be on the front lines, manhandling crooks and responding to calls anymore."

Michael leaned in to whisper something in my ear, and Detective Preston's voice caught us both by surprise.

"Michael," she hissed, "not in the office. People around here think I slept my way to the top. You don't want the same for your current girlfriend, do you?" I turned to her, surprised. "No hard feelings, Sarconi," she said to me. "You've found yourself a good guy. Hang on to him." Regret passed over her face before she walked away.

"What was that about?" I whispered.

"I'll tell you one of these days. Now go see what Peterson wants and get out of here. You don't want to go out on tour, do you?"

"Fine."

I knocked on Peterson's door, and he gestured me inside. "Take a seat, Sarconi." He picked up an official looking form. "How was the exam?"

"I don't know."

He nodded a few times. "I'm sure you did well. Assuming you placed high enough and a promotion is in order, I thought I'd let you know, Detective Lightman's already put in a request to have you transferred to his unit."

"Sir?"

"I know it's premature. Typically, the top of the list gets their pick of assignments, based on availability and openings. Depending on how you ranked, you may have something else in mind, but I wanted you to be aware of his request." Peterson scratched his chin. "Would you be interested in taking it?"

"I...uh..."

Peterson held up his hand. "I get it. You may have your sights set on RHD or vice."

"Not vice," I said.

"But you have no interest in gangs?"

"I never said that."

"Okay, well, I just wanted you to keep that in mind. Whatever you did, you impressed Lightman, and that isn't an easy feat. That alone tells me you're going to make a great detective."

"Thank you, sir."

After running into a couple of friends who asked how I was, I went back to Michael's desk. He was on the phone. I ran my hand along his shoulder as my silent way of saying goodbye. He covered the mouthpiece and said, "I'll see you later?"

"Absolutely." I took a few steps toward the door before turning back around. "I'm not sure if you had anything to do with it, but tell Jack, if I passed, I'll take it."

Break-ins and Bouquets

Don't miss the third book in the Lexie Sarconi series, Compromised Undercover.

When Officer Lexie Sarconi transferred out of vice, she never thought they'd send her back, especially after making detective and finding a new home with the gangs unit. But now she's walking the streets in a pair of fishnets and a miniskirt. Detective Michael Riley's been sent on a deep cover assignment that he can't or won't tell her about. Not only is she worried about Riley's safety, but she's also worried about their relationship.

The setback's supposed to be temporary. So why is Riley meeting his ex in a trashy hotel? Lexie can't think about that now. The entire police department has been tasked with cracking down on crime, and the john she just arrested doesn't exist, at least not on paper.

The deeper she delves into his phony background, the more anxious the police brass become. This arrest is huge, and every department wants a piece of this guy. But he wants a piece of her.

ABOUT THE AUTHOR

G.K. Parks is the author of the Alexis Parker series. The first novel, *Likely Suspects,* tells the story of Alexis' first foray into the private sector.

G.K. Parks received a Bachelor of Arts in Political Science and History. After spending some time in law school, G.K. changed paths and earned a Master of Arts in Criminology/Criminal Justice. Now all that education is being put to use creating a fictional world based upon years of study and research.

Elisa Archer has always loved reading, writing, and romance. On most days you can find her hiding behind a computer screen, frantically typing away at her latest story. She's always been an avid reader and enjoys everything from technothrillers to steamy romance. In fact, there isn't a genre of book she doesn't like. Writing just seemed to be the natural progression of her passion for books.

You can find additional information by visiting our website at
www.gkparks.com

Sign up for the e-mail newsletter for the latest information on upcoming releases, sales, free promotions, and more.
www.gkparks.com/newsletter